She jerked and looked up.

Archer had been in her condo twice now in the span of six weeks. It was a record. And she was far less shocked to see him than she ought to have been.

"What are you doing here?"

He held up a package wrapped with brown kraft paper and twine. "A care package from Meredith for Ros. Only since she hasn't bothered informing anyone of her new address, I don't know where to take it."

"Could have taken it to her office," Nell pointed out waspishly.

"Yeah, but then I wouldn't have an excuse to see your cheerful face. You know, anyone and their mother's brother could walk in through your open front door."

"Anyone *did*."

"I'm not just anyone."

She gave him a look. "Seriously. What do you *want*?"

"Seriously, maybe I don't *want* anything. That so hard to believe?"

It wasn't, and that should have been a relief. So why did his words cause her heart to sink to her stomach in disappointment?

* * *

RETURN TO THE DOUBLE C:
Under the big blue Wyoming sky,
this family discovers true love!

Dear Reader,

Why is it that it takes *so* long for some people to just...get...a...clue?

As usual, from an observer's standpoint, that is an easy question with a shake-one's-head response. From the perspective of the individual or individuals involved? Not such an easy thing.

Such is the case for Nell and Archer. They've known one another for a very long time. Occasionally danced around their mutual attraction. More often preferred to stick their heads in the sand.

But nature tends to shake things out, including truths that may or may not be easy to face. Nell, who has trusted her head over her heart for all of her adult life, learns that life is so much better when she finally starts listening to her heart. Because when it comes to Archer and the things that really are true, her heart has always had the "clue."

Allison

Lawfully Unwed

ALLISON LEIGH

HARLEQUIN
SPECIAL
EDITION

HARLEQUIN®
SPECIAL EDITION™

ISBN-13: 978-1-335-89471-7

Lawfully Unwed

Copyright © 2020 by Allison Lee Johnson

This edition published by arrangement with Harlequin Books S.A.

For questions and comments about the quality of this book, please contact us at CustomerService@Harlequin.com.

Harlequin Enterprises ULC
22 Adelaide St. West, 40th Floor
Toronto, Ontario M5H 4E3, Canada
www.Harlequin.com

Printed in U.S.A.

Though her name is frequently on bestseller lists, **Allison Leigh**'s high point as a writer is hearing from readers that they laughed, cried or lost sleep while reading her books. She credits her family with great patience for the time she's parked at her computer, and for blessing her with the kind of love she wants her readers to share with the characters living in the pages of her books. Contact her at allisonleigh.com.

For Amanda and Chad with all of my love.

Chapter One

"Delicious cake, Nell."

"It's going to be a great year, Nell."

"Don't look a day older, Nell."

With a smile that felt wooden on her face, Nell Brewster returned hugs as the well-wishers departed The Wet Bar one after another.

Fortunately, there weren't as many people at the pub as Nell's best friend, Rosalind, had expected. She was the one who'd insisted on the party for Nell. Her reasoning was that Friday afternoon on a holiday weekend would be perfect. Prime time for their crowd to escape their offices for a little more R&R before the long weekend. The July

Fourth holiday—on the coming Monday—meant no court proceedings until Tuesday.

"It's not every day a girl turns thirty-six," Ros had said on a laugh not even a month ago when she'd emailed the invitations.

Thank God for that, is what Nell had thought. At the time, she'd been thinking only about becoming another year older and feeling like she was spinning the same wheels she'd been spinning for years.

Now, as far as birthdays went, she couldn't have imagined a worse one. If she could have skipped the celebration altogether, she would have.

Ros had—a fact that had earned more than a few comments.

Instead of telling the truth behind her absence, Nell had just let everyone assume that her friend was stuck on a case. Anyone who knew Ros knew that she wasn't the type who would have escaped for an early holiday celebration if she still had work to do. She was too devoted to her career.

And why not? Rosalind Pastore was the heir apparent at her father's law firm. She'd just been made a partner. Working was a reasonable excuse for her absence that afternoon, and a far more preferable one than the truth.

That was going to come out soon enough.

The legal community in Cheyenne—in the

entire state of Wyoming for that matter—was a tight one.

Nell suffered through a final hug from Scott Muelhaupt—the newest associate at Pastore Legal—as he wished her a happy birthday for what felt like the tenth time. He hugged her longer than necessary, but she supposed he figured he had a right to, given the fact that they'd been casually dating for several weeks now.

"Sure I can't take you out somewhere for dinner?" He smiled hopefully. He was a nice-looking guy. Decent. He smelled clean and he even took his mother out for dinner every Sunday afternoon.

He just didn't make any real bells ring for Nell, much less any cymbals crash.

She wondered if he'd be as interested in her once word got out that she'd quit her job at Pastore Legal. Or if he, like Ros—with whom she'd been friends forever—would decide it was time to cut all ties. If he—again like Ros—would land on the other side of the line that had been drawn in the sand between Nell and Martin Pastore.

Martin. The founder of Pastore Legal. Champion of the people.

As long as the "people" weren't an associate named Nell Brewster.

Quit or be fired.

Those had been her choices. She'd figured that

out quickly enough even though she hadn't been so quick to see everything else.

She hated knowing how oblivious she'd been. Hated knowing that she'd been such an easy pawn. Really, *really* hated facing the fact that for so long she'd put her trust where it didn't belong.

At thirty-six, she was no smarter than she'd been at twenty-six. Or sixteen, for that matter.

"I'm sure." She slid off the seat where she'd been tensely perched as those who *had* stopped by for birthday cake and adult beverages said their goodbyes, and kept the tall metal-backed stool between them. Casually dating a work associate was fine and dandy. Until it wasn't. "Thanks, though."

Scott shrugged, ever good-natured. "Next time."

She kept her wooden smile in place as she waved toward the slab of cake that remained on the long table. "Take some cake. There's plenty."

It was sized for the crowd Ros had initially expected. The crowd that hadn't panned out.

At another time, the two of them would have laughed about it, just figuring that left more cake and wine for them. Neither of which was ever a bad thing.

But it wasn't another time.

Still, what was a copious amount of leftover cake when the rest of Nell's life had landed in such an unexpected mess?

No job.

No best friend.

She stifled a sigh, then nearly jumped out of her skin when a tall man brushed against her as he took the barstool next to hers and greeted the bartender by name.

She automatically shifted aside with a murmured apology, but pressed her lips together when she realized who the man was.

Well, this was just the icing on the cake, wasn't it? Proof that she really *was* oblivious.

One portion of her pathetic mind heard the newcomer order a drink while the rest of her bristled with fresh awareness.

It was always that way when it came to Archer Templeton.

Bristling nerves. Bristling irritation. Bristling…whatever.

The last time she'd seen him had been almost a month ago, in a small courtroom several hours away from Cheyenne.

Now, before she could even ask what he was doing here, Archer turned to her, the squat glass Cheri the bartender had given him clasped in his long, square-tipped fingers and said, "Happy birthday, Cornelia." His lips were curved slightly as he lifted the glass in a toast.

Even though she knew better, she couldn't help feeling a secret thrill at the notion that he was there at The Wet Bar because of *her*. Her pulse quickened, and she felt a vague but inevitable cymbal crash. And it annoyed the daylights out of her. "Why are *you* here?"

The faint lines arrowing out from his vivid green eyes deepened with obvious amusement. "Ah, Nell." He waved his whiskey glass slightly in the direction of the table and the leftover cake. "Is it too hard to believe I'm here to wish an old friend a happy birthday?"

She steeled herself against the charm that he'd no doubt been radiating since birth. He'd certainly had it ever since they met half her lifetime ago. But it was dangerous to be sucked into that charm. She'd had too many of her own court cases decimated because of Archer's charm, which made it so easy to forget how fiercely brilliant he was.

"Yes." She narrowed her eyes at him. "You've heard, haven't you." It wasn't a question. "*That's* why you're here."

His tawny eyebrows rose a fraction. "Heard what? That you and Muelhaupt are a thing?" he goaded, his eyes glinting. "You always did go for the mousy type. What's he in charge of again at Pastore Legal? Keeping the flowers fresh in the conference room?"

Her jaw tightened. Scott was a very competent tax lawyer and she knew the more she defended him to Archer, the more he'd make of it. And Archer never had anything good to say about her law firm and particularly the man who'd founded it. "Go away, Archer."

He smiled and a dimple flashed in his lean cheek. "Is that any way to treat an old friend?"

She dragged her eyes away from the dimple and the cheek. Not without noticing it was smooth. Freshly shaven. Which meant he had probably been in court that day. Otherwise, he would have sported the unshaven look.

She'd seen him both ways so many times over the years and it was a toss-up which was more appealing.

And now, because of him, she felt too warm in her suit jacket. And she'd rather chew glass than let it show. "Just because we've known each other for years doesn't mean we're old friends." Her voice was flat. "You're just Ros's brother." Stepbrother, technically.

Was it her imagination or had his smoothly charming smile become a fraction less smooth? He lifted his hand and tucked an escaped curl behind her ear. "Your understanding is as faulty as your allegiance to Martin Pastore," he drawled, with the usual anti-Pastore edge in his voice.

Then his hand dropped away and he lifted his glass again in salute.

Only the salute wasn't for her any more than the relaxed smile that crossed his face was. The aim was off entirely. Instead, both were directed toward a smashingly attractive blonde who was crossing toward Archer, a brilliant smile on her beautiful face.

Her name was Taylor Potts. *Judge* Taylor Potts.

Nell hid a grimace as the judge offered her cheek for Archer to kiss when he stood to greet her. She settled her palm on his chest with the familiarity of a lover. "Sorry I'm late," she practically purred. "Got caught up on a new ethics case. Hope I was worth the wait."

Nell practically choked. She slid back onto the barstool she'd nearly abandoned just minutes ago and caught the bartender's eye as she turned her back on the couple. "I'll take that champagne now," she said, trying with all of her might to tune out Archer and his judge.

Of course he hadn't come to The Wet Bar because of Nell.

The bartender held up the bottle that she hadn't wanted earlier. The bottle that had been a gift from Ros.

She nodded and waved her hand in invitation to pour a glass. "That's the one, Cheri. Open up that puppy," she said with false brightness.

After all. It's not every day a girl turns thirty-six.

"You sure I can't talk you into coming with me?" Taylor angled her lovely head as she smiled up at Archer.

It had been several hours since they'd shared a drink at The Wet Bar. After they'd left, they'd had dinner at the most expensive restaurant in Cheyenne. There was nothing fast about the service at Clever Bacie's and Archer would have preferred a steak dinner to the Asian fusion cuisine, but it was Taylor's favorite place and the food was good.

He'd always enjoyed her company. She was smart. Funny. Attractive. And had been as disinterested in serious ties as he'd been.

Until lately.

He was thirty-nine years old. He recognized the signs.

"Sorry," he said, and he actually was. Because he'd miss their easy, no-ties relationship. "I've got to be in Braden early in the morning." It was the truth. His hometown was several hours away.

Even when she made a face, she did it beautifully. "Well, a rain check, then."

He smiled noncommittally and opened her car door for her. "Drive careful."

He heard her faint sigh, though the smile on her face didn't fade as she sank into the driver's seat of her luxury sedan. "Will I hear from you next week?"

"If I'm in town." He leaned down and brushed a kiss over her cheek.

"Gage Stanton needing you again in Colorado?"

"Gage isn't the only one I do business with in Denver," Archer reminded her, though it was true the real estate developer had paid the lion's share of Archer's billable hours over the last few years. Most recently because of a hotly contested property on Rambling Mountain near Weaver, also several hours north of Cheyenne. Braden and Weaver, situated about thirty miles apart, were both small towns. But together, they managed to meet the needs of the residents in their region and if Gage's plan to develop a resort came to pass, it would change the tourism landscape altogether for both communities. "I *do* have a practice in Denver."

"And a few others spread across Wyoming," she said wryly. "I don't remember you being so ambitious back in our law school days."

He chuckled. "I don't remember you aspiring to be a judge, either."

She shrugged. "What can I say? Legal aid is satisfying but it's hard to pay the bills on that sort of wage." She pushed a button and her car started, the window rolled down, her seat automatically adjusted and a soft voice began reciting her schedule for the day.

"Particularly bills that come with cars like this." He closed her door for her and backed away.

Her smile widened and with a light wave, she drove away.

He blew out a breath and started walking down the street to where his truck was parked outside The Wet Bar. When he reached it, though, he didn't get in.

Instead, he stood there on the sidewalk, dithering like some damn fool.

"Be smart, Arch," he muttered aloud, not caring that he earned a startled glance from an older couple walking past. Nell hadn't appreciated his making an appearance for her birthday earlier. If she were still inside—and that was a pretty large *if*—she wouldn't feel any differently now.

He was supposed to be in Braden early in the morning. Not because of the Rambling Mountain deal—that was currently on pause, tangled in the red tape that Gage Stanton was paying him to untangle—but because his sister Greer expected all hands to be on deck for her son Finn's first birthday party.

Archer hadn't been home in nearly a month. He didn't have a problem helping out even though he knew there were plenty of other able-bodied and willing helpers Greer could count on.

He pivoted on his heel and pulled out his keys to unlock the truck.

He'd known Nell in law school, too. She and Ros had been just starting out when he and Taylor had been finishing. He'd known Nell even before that, though, thanks to her friendship with Ros.

She'd accompanied his stepsister to Braden one summer during one of Ros's forced visits with her mother.

Nell, whose mother had recently died, had seemed to enjoy the time more than Ros had. His stepsister hadn't been there because she wanted to be. She'd been there only because she had to be. Ordinarily, Ros lived with her dad, Martin, in Cheyenne and wanted nothing to do with her mother or the family that Meredith had made with Archer's dad in Braden.

Be smart, Arch.

He pocketed the keys, turned back around and crossed the sidewalk in long strides. He doubted Nell would still be there. Once he confirmed that, he'd go back to his place, grab his bag and drive on out to Braden tonight. There was always somewhere to sleep at his folks' place, even though it might be on the couch if they were on grandparent duty watching one of his sisters' kids.

And if, by chance, she *were* still inside—

He entered the pub, which was a lot more crowded now than it had been hours earlier. A lot more raucous, too, with classic Stones on the jukebox vying to be heard over voices and laughter.

But there was no sign of Nell; he couldn't make out her tightly knotted dark hair or boxy gray suit among the crowd. The table where the cake and gift bags had been was now covered in beer bottles and surrounded by several good ol' boys obviously out for a good time as they shouted encouragement to a trio of ladies dancing for all they were worth in one corner.

That wasn't disappointment he felt.

Nope.

Just relief.

Keys in hand once more, he turned to go, waiting as a gaggle of kids who barely looked old enough to drive, much less drink, shuffled inside. While he stood there, a peal of high-pitched laughter rose above the jukebox and he glanced over his shoulder toward the source just in time to see a couple of the good ol' boys helping the dancing ladies up onto the bar top.

Last time Archer remembered anyone dancing on a bar top, he'd been in college. Smiling ruefully because he suddenly felt like he'd gotten old, he reached for the door before it swung closed after the kids entered. Another edgy laugh rose above the general din and he glanced over at the dancers again.

And stood stock-still.

The loud voices and the louder music dimmed.

The swinging door knocked into his shoulder.

"Dude, mind if we—" The kid wanting to get past him broke off, his Adam's apple bobbing when Archer's attention slid from the woman dancing on the bar to him. "Sorry," he muttered and turned the other direction.

Archer didn't pay him any mind and entered the fray, pushing his way through the people crowded inside the pub, aiming for the bar. Maybe it was the fact that he stood several inches above six feet. Maybe it was the frown he could feel on his face. Whatever it was, people moved aside and he reached the bar in a matter of seconds.

He reached up and grabbed Nell's wrist. "What the hell are you doing?" His voice was swallowed by the hoots and hollers that were rising in scale by the second, thanks to the gyrations of the women on the bar. One of them had even yanked off her T-shirt and was dancing in just her bra and a short denim skirt.

Fortunately, Nell wasn't that far gone. Yeah, the shapeless jacket of her suit was nowhere to be seen, but at least her silky sleeveless blouse was still where it belonged.

Was it any wonder he hadn't noticed her at first?

No jacket. No shoes. Her hair let out of that godforsaken knot she always sported and springing down beyond her shoulders.

She shook off his hand with an annoyed glare. "Go away!" She twirled again and the hem of her plain skirt slapped him in the face.

"Thatagirl," someone hooted when the second

woman tore off her shirt and swung it around her head.

Archer caught Cheri's eye. "It's just a matter of time before the cops come," he said loudly, leaning toward her so she could hear.

The bartender shrugged helplessly. "Won't be the first time," she shouted back.

Archer grimaced. He tried to catch Nell's hand again, but she wasn't having any of that. Her cheeks were flushed, her dark eyes wild.

He leaned toward Cheri again. "How much has she had?"

"I didn't think it was enough for that." She turned away to stick another glass under the taps.

Archer followed Nell as she danced her way along the bar. "Where's Ros?"

He knew that Nell heard him because her eyes skated over his before she spun away again.

Only this time her bare foot slipped on a wet spot and she started to fall.

His heart shot up into his throat and he barely caught her before she toppled over the edge. He grunted when her elbow caught him on the nose and he muttered an apology to the stunned woman he nearly unseated when he caught Nell.

Nell, who wasn't showing the least bit of gratitude that he'd prevented her from tumbling head over heels right onto the floor of The Wet Bar with what seemed like half the town's population looking on.

"Leggoame," she slurred, pushing ineffectually at his hands.

"You're drunk." He set her on her feet but grabbed her arms when her knees failed to do their job and she swayed wildly.

"Amnot." Her head lolled against his arm when he slid it behind her back. She looked up at him, but her eyes—dark as chocolate drops—were unfocused. Her dark hair was a riot of curls clinging to her cheeks and the long column of her neck. "Jushavinfun." Her eyes rolled slightly but she jerked herself upright. "Issmybirthday," she announced as if it were news.

"Where's Ros?" he asked again.

Nell's forehead wrinkled. Her lips pinched together. Those chocolate-drop eyes suddenly gleamed wetly. "Snothere."

"I can see that." He renewed his grip around her shoulders and looked toward Cheri again. "Jacket? Purse?"

The bartender jerked her chin. "Behind here. Just give me a sec."

"Why *isn't* she here? You two never miss celebrating each other's birthdays."

"Haddafight."

Surprise jerked at him. He knew *he* had plenty of fights with his stepsister—they hadn't been able to agree on the time of day from the moment his father had married her mother.

Nell was sniffing hard as if she was trying not to cry.

"About what?"

Her lips moved and he almost thought she was going to tell him. But the days of her confiding in him were long gone, and instead, annoyance suddenly crossed her face again. She pushed against him. "Lemmego. I can stand."

It was easy to evade her puny efforts. "Sure you can. I'll let you go as soon as I pour you into a cab to go home."

The tears came back and she looked even more miserable. Which was saying something.

"Toldyou. Haddafight. Can't." She shook her head.

As far as Archer could tell, that just made her sway even more dizzily. He caught her around the waist, trying not to remember the last time he'd held her so closely. That had also been a long time ago. Too long ago to still be so vivid in his mind. She was thinner now. Not a lot, because she'd always been slender. But—

"Here's her stuff." Cheri interrupted his thoughts, pushing a bundle of dull gray fabric and an oversize purse into his other arm. "No idea about her shoes."

"Thasmapurse," Nell observed.

Cheri gave Archer a dry look. "Better get moving," she warned, cocking her head to one side. "Think I hear the siren."

Archer wasn't particularly concerned about the police. But he knew Nell would regret getting caught up in the fray once she was sober. Her fall from the bar hadn't stopped the other two women from dancing, and a dozen people had begun pounding their fists on the bar in tempo with the drums.

He decided her missing shoes weren't worth the time it would take to find them and he hitched her up once more around the waist as he headed toward the door. It wasn't all that easy when she seemed determined to go the other way, but he prevailed, finally pushing through the doorway and getting her out onto the sidewalk, where the police siren was close enough to be deafening. Blue-and-red lights danced over the vehicles parked at the curb.

Including his own truck.

The sound of the siren at least seemed to quell Nell's efforts to escape and she didn't fight him when Archer lifted her up into the truck. "If you don't want to go back to the condo, where *do* you want to go?" He braced himself to hear Muelhaupt's name, but she didn't say anything.

She just shook her head again, looking sad and pale and pathetic.

He didn't need Nell Brewster tugging at his heartstrings. *Those* days were supposed to be long gone, too.

"Fine," he muttered, and yanked the seat belt around her, clicking it into place. There was no point in calling his stepsister on Nell's behalf. Ros always took her sweet-ass time returning his calls. Which was one of the reasons why he generally went with the in-person route with her, despite the fact that it annoyed her no end. "Hotel it is."

Nell didn't react. Her eyes were closed.

When he closed the door, she leaned heavily against it, and her cheek smashed inelegantly against the window.

If he weren't so concerned, he would have been amused. Would have considered snapping a shot of her on his cell phone just for the pleasure of tormenting her with the image some day off in the future.

But Nell had never been one to tie one on.

She'd always been too uptight for that.

He quickly rounded the truck and sketched a wave at the police officers who were now leaving their vehicle and heading quickly toward The Wet Bar.

"Hey, Arch." The senior partner—a woman named Donna Rhodes—greeted him with a resigned look. "You coming from in there?"

"Yeah. Probably over occupancy, but nobody's naked and nobody's fighting."

"Yet." That came from the younger partner—a guy named Marcus Welby. He was so young that Archer couldn't help but wonder if his parents were aware they'd named him after an iconic television character from decades past. "Place is dull as ditchwater on weekdays but come the weekends?"

The two officers entered the bar as a second patrol car pulled up with its lights also flashing.

Archer didn't hang around to see what would happen next. He got in the truck and left the scene before it had a chance to actually become a scene.

When he was a couple of blocks away where the sirens weren't as loud, he pulled over again at the side of the road and nudged Nell's shoulder with his fingertips. "Hey. You conscious over there?"

Her answer was a resounding snore.

He sat back and exhaled. "Well, hell, Arch. Now what are you going to do?"

Chapter Two

Her mouth tasted like a rabbit had taken up residence inside, and maybe even decided to die there, too. Her eyes felt gritty—too gritty to dare trying to open. Her dry lips matched the dire condition inside her mouth. And her head…oh, the pain in her head was something to behold.

Nell groaned, grimaced and gingerly rolled onto her side. At least the pillow was smooth and wonderfully cool against her cheek as she hugged it close and tried to block out all of the wholly unpleasant sensations involved with waking.

For a brief moment she had a vague thought she

might have the flu. But memory surfaced quickly enough. She didn't have a virus. She wasn't sick.

She was paying the price for drowning her miseries the night before in a veritable vat of alcohol.

She snuggled her face deeper into the cool, squishy pillow, seeking comfort and escape from the hideous hangover.

How long had it been since she'd suffered even a fraction of this misery? Five years? Ten? There'd been a lot of cocktails at Ros's thirty-fifth birthday the year before, but—

Ros.

Nell rolled onto her back and sighed, though it came out more like a groan. She and Ros just needed to clear the air. They'd been friends for so long that Nell couldn't imagine her life without Ros in it. She was the only "family" that Nell even had. Her and Martin.

Her head pounded anew at the thought. He'd been a father figure to her, whether he'd ever intended to be or not. He had certainly been her mentor when it came to the law. If it hadn't been for him, she'd have never even gotten into law school. Instead, she'd probably still be working at a used-book store.

She gingerly rubbed her aching forehead, knuckled her eyes, then after a quick, bracing breath, shoved back the covers and swung her bare feet off the bed.

Instead of feeling the warmth of soft sculptured carpet under her toes, though, she encountered a solid surface. A cold, smooth, solid surface.

Her eyes flew open despite the grittiness and she squinted against the light streaming through the mullioned windows next to the bed.

Her bedroom had carpeted floors. And it definitely did not have mullioned windows.

Horror was congealing inside her stomach and she breathed carefully, very afraid that she was going to be sick.

Where was she?

There wasn't one single thing about the bedroom that was familiar. Not the floor—a deep brown wood, she saw through her slitted eyes—or the navy blue sheets and pillowcases on the bed. The nightstand next to the wide, wide bed—hers was the same full-size thing she'd owned since college—was also wood. Good, solid, maybe even an antique. It didn't quite match the massive dresser across the room from the bed, but it coordinated well. Nothing sat on the top of the nightstand except an angular Tiffany-style lamp.

Her stomach roiling, she cautiously slid from the bed, tugging the hem of her silky tank into place. She was still wearing her blouse from last night, as well as her skirt. Surely that was a good sign.

It was bad enough to wake up in a place she

didn't recognize. But at least she wasn't naked to boot. *That* would bring on a whole new height of alarm.

And she already felt like she was perched on the platform of a high dive.

She took a cautious step on the wood floor, freezing in place when it emitted a soft creak.

She listened intently for a sound in response from beyond the closed bedroom door, but couldn't hear a thing. Maybe because her head was already filled with the sound of her heart. It was pounding so hard it seemed to reverberate through her chest as well as her aching head.

She realized she was holding her breath when she started to feel dizzy, and she exhaled shakily, which also sounded excessively loud. She took another step. This one was unaccompanied by a creaking floorboard. Then another. And another until she reached the dresser and the silver-framed photo next to a jumble of coins and a half-empty pack of chewing gum.

Her hand was shaking as she carefully reached for the photo to angle it so she could see what it was, but despite all the care she took, she still managed to fumble with the frame and it slid into the change, knocking several pennies and quarters off the side of the dresser. She swore under her breath, hearing the ping as the coins hit the floor and bounced and rolled. She grabbed the picture with both hands, holding it down on the dresser as if the thing were in danger of taking flight.

Considering her clumsiness, maybe it was.

Still, there was no noise from beyond the bedroom door. Feeling weak with relief, alarm and outright disgust with herself, she rested her elbows on the dresser and sucked in unsteady breaths as she studied the photo. It was an old one. She was making that judgment based on the style of clothing the pretty blonde woman wore. She was holding a baby who could have been a boy or a girl—the yellow blanket it was wrapped in gave no clue.

Nell propped her aching head in her hand and closed her eyes again.

Should she just straighten her spine and leave the room to find out where on earth she was? Or should she snoop some more and gird herself with more knowledge before she opened the door?

Snooping was sort of in her nature.

She was a lawyer, after all.

Her fingers toyed with the pull on the dresser drawer. She tugged lightly and the drawer slid open an inch. Another inch. All she gained was a glimpse of white before she heard a thump outside the door that had her hastily closing the drawer.

She whirled so that her back was to the dresser, hiding her shaking hands behind her, and watched the door while her heart hammered and her stomach skittered around uneasily.

She flinched as though she'd been struck when there was a soft knock on the door. One, two, three of them in a quick little row.

Knock-knock-knock.

She chewed the inside of her lip, her breath building and building against the dam inside her chest.

"Nell?" The voice as well as the knock was still soft.

It was also distinctively male.

She clenched her teeth and frowned. The voice was male. Scott's? She was embarrassed even more that she couldn't tell for sure. She'd never been to his place, but if this *was* his home, maybe she wouldn't have to feel quite so annoyed with herself.

They were dating. More or less. She hadn't slept with him, though he'd made it plain he was interested.

Her gaze slid guiltily to the bed. The bedding was tumbled. The pillows askew.

Had she slept with him? The state of the bed didn't give any clue at all.

She rubbed her forehead. Scott had left the bar the night before, though. She didn't remember him returning. But then again, she didn't remember a lot of—

"Nell?" The deep voice and the knock were a little louder this time. "You awake yet?"

Scott's voice wasn't that deep. Was it?

She shook her head, wishing this was a really bad and really realistic dream. She could feel the ridges of the well-preserved wood beneath her feet, for goodness' sake!

She stared at the door handle, her mind dancing fatalistically among the nonsensical thoughts, when the voice caused a spark.

A sudden, quick, awful spark of familiarity.

"No." She shook her head. "No, absolutely *no*."

But the doorknob was turning, and she watched it as though the worst sort of slow-motion nightmare she had ever endured was unfolding. Then the door swung open to reveal the owner of the voice.

His green eyes were brilliant and showed no signs whatsoever of his having tied one on the night before. And when he spotted her standing there all frozen with her backside pressed against the drawer she'd peeked into, he arched one of his tawny eyebrows slightly. "Well, well, well, Cornelia," Archer drawled. "You *are* awake."

"You!" Accusation flooded her voice.

His other eyebrow rose, too. "What'd I do?"

She knew her mouth was gaping like a water-starved fish's. "What *didn't* you do?"

He shrugged, which only drew her attention

to the breadth of his shoulders beneath the plain white undershirt he was wearing.

He padded barefoot into the room and set the breakfast tray he was holding on top of the dresser. "I'm sure you'll tell me in several dozen more paragraphs than necessary." He lifted one of the plain brown mugs from the tray and extended it toward her. "Assume you still like it light and sweet?"

She dragged her eyes up from the slouchy navy-colored pajama pants hanging precariously on his very male hips. "What?"

"Coffee." He pushed the mug into her numb hand and wrapped her fingers around it. "Don't drop the mug. It's one of the last ones I have of hers."

She was having a hard time putting two coherent thoughts together. Not only had he brought coffee, but there was also a stack of golden toast sitting on a paper plate and a jar of jam with a knife sticking out of it.

Cymbals were crashing, and not necessarily inside her head. The only thing she knew for sure was that whatever was going on here, it was his fault. Knowing it was an uncharitable thought—he *had* made toast, after all—didn't stop her from having it. "Hers?"

"My mother." He tapped the photo frame before putting a finger beneath her hand to nudge it—

and the mug—upward toward her lips. "Drink. You'll feel better."

She actually took a sip of the coffee, which had exactly the right amount of cream and sugar, before she determinedly set the mug back on the tray. Considering everything, it was a minor miracle she didn't spill it or drop it. "What have you done? Why am I here?"

He leaned leisurely against the doorjamb and cradled his mug in his wide palm. "I'm wounded." He sounded mildly amused. The corners of his sinfully shaped lips curved upward. "You don't remember? And here I've landed myself in the doghouse with my sister for choosing you over my nephew's birthday."

"No I do *not* remember." She shoved her tangled hair away from her eyes, the better to glare at him. "Obviously." She drew out the word with what Ros—a diehard *Harry Potter* fan—had long ago termed Nell's best Snape-ishness.

His green eyes seemed to gain an extra sparkle as they traveled from the mop that her hair must resemble, down over her wrinkled silk tank and even more wrinkled skirt, to her toes that were actually clenching against the wood floor.

Her cheeks felt hot. Naturally, she needed a pedicure in the worst way, too. She hadn't made her last standing appointment with Renée because of a filing Martin had—

It all came tumbling down on her again, managing to supplant even the worry over what had occurred here last night.

Martin's betrayal.

The argument with Ros.

Her recent change from being among the gainfully employed.

The weight of it all slammed down on her shoulders, making her slump.

Every muscle and joint and hair follicle aching, she sank down on the edge of the bed, then just as hurriedly pushed off it again.

The bed belonged to Archer Templeton. She had no idea at all how she'd come to be sleeping in it, whether she was still fully clothed or not. She knew the man from old, and he was cleverer than the devil himself.

She snatched a piece of his gum from the dresser, peeled off the foil and shoved it into her mouth to banish the deceased Mr. Cottontail. Then she steeled herself to brush past him to leave the room. Not that she knew where she was headed, but anywhere was better than the bedroom.

As soon as she was in the hall, she spotted the staircase and aimed straight for it. She pounded down the steps as though Archer was at her heels, even though he wasn't. She felt breathless and even more nauseated when she reached the bottom. The living room was straight ahead. The kitchen to the right. She turned left and fortunately found the powder room.

She slammed the door, locked it and spent several minutes hanging over the sink while cold water ran over her wrists until she felt a little better.

Oh, her head still felt as heavy as a bowling ball with loose rocks clanging around inside, but at least she didn't think she'd vomit on her poorly maintained pedicure.

She wrapped the gum in a square of tissue paper and tossed it in the small gold trash can in the corner next to the vintage pedestal sink that—knowing Archer—was probably an original. He was the most annoying person she'd ever met, but he'd always had impeccable taste. No reproductions—no matter how excellent—for him.

She cupped water in her hands and rinsed her mouth, then splashed more water over her face. When she straightened again, her reflection in the oval mirror over the sink was genuinely frightening but at least her eyes didn't look as bleary as she felt. She raked her fingers through her hair, spreading the dampness beyond her hairline, and longed for a clip or hair tie, but—like everything else in her life at the moment—no luck.

She adjusted her skirt so the vent was once more in the back where it belonged and tucked in her blouse. Barefoot and jacketless or not, she couldn't very well hibernate in Archer's elegant little powder room.

She straightened her shoulders and left the room.

He had come downstairs and was now sprawled in a leather chair, without a care in the world, coffee mug still cupped in his wide palm.

His smooth jawline of the night before was now shadowed in a golden-brown stubble and his thick, gilded hair tumbled over his forehead.

He was the most annoying man she knew and the most attractive. Still.

Didn't it just figure?

With no small amount of relief, she spotted her oversize purse sitting on a table in the foyer and pounced on it. "Shoes?"

"God only knows."

Her stomach churned all over again. Not because of a lost pair of shoes. But because losing them at all was just more evidence of behavior she couldn't recall.

Her fingers were shaking as she pulled her cell phone from her purse where it was tucked in its usual pocket. The battery was nearly dead and she had a couple of dozen notifications for new messages. She ignored them as she sent a request for a rideshare. Without looking at Archer again, she went out the front door.

He had a wooden garden bench sitting on the

porch beneath the wide mullioned windows of the living room. She perched on the edge of it while she dug in her purse for her sunglasses.

They afforded her clanging head with a small bit of ease when she put them on.

Her knuckles were white around her phone as she watched the progress of her rideshare on the screen, praying for all she was worth that the car would arrive before Archer decided to come out and torment her some more.

He had the ability to do that simply by breathing the same air as her. It wouldn't have been so problematic, except that he was perfectly aware of the effect he had.

At least he had been back in the day.

Still, it remained a good reason to avoid him.

The clock on her phone told her it was almost noon. She had no sense of how long she'd slept, except that it hadn't been long enough.

She lifted her sunglasses enough to rub her eyes, and then consulted her phone app again. The ride was around the corner.

She breathed a little easier now that it was almost here, because she was certain she could feel Archer's eyes drilling into her through the window. She just hoped he didn't come out onto the porch. She pushed off the bench, dragging the strap of her purse over her shoulder, and walked barefoot down the shallow brick steps. She crossed the neat patch of summer-green grass and wondered if Archer actually mowed it himself.

And wondering *that* annoyed her, too.

She marched a little more briskly from the grass to the sidewalk and toward the corner where a little hybrid vehicle had just come into view. She waved her arm, flagging it down, and peered into the window, making certain the driver matched the one on her app. She did, so Nell opened the back door, tossed her purse inside and folded herself in after it.

"Morning." The driver was a gray-haired woman with a cheerful chirpy voice. She read off Nell's home address. "That's where we're heading, yeah?"

Nell closed her eyes and pressed her head against the seat back. "Yes. Thanks," she added a little belatedly once the car lurched into motion. It felt odd the way the vehicle moved along so silently without the noise and feel of a typical gas engine. "How does this thing run in the winter?"

The driver gave another chirp of laughter. "Going to have to wait until this winter to see. I just bought her." She tapped her hand against the steering wheel. "She's a good girl, though. Hasn't failed me yet." She slowed and turned the corner again. "Get a lot of looks from other people, though. Not quite the usual sight yet here in Cheyenne."

"Or the rest of Wyoming," Nell surmised.

The driver laughed again. "Of course, ride-sharing is still pretty new to most folks around here, too." Her cheerful tone was soothing. "Even though it really isn't. I've been doing it nearly five years now."

"Guess you must like it."

"Sure. I can work as much or as little as I want. And the money's better than you might think. I earn more doing this than I did even after twenty-five years in mortgage banking. And retirement is too boring for me." She laughed. "For now, anyway. I like filling my time. What do you do?"

"I'm a lawyer." Nell rubbed a finger against the throbbing in her forehead.

"Mind if I ask where? Person never knows when they might find themselves in need of one."

Nell's lips twisted. "I'm evaluating things at the moment."

"Ah." The driver nodded sagely. "Well, if you need a little financial boost during the evaluation period, I can recommend my company. Decisions sometimes come easier when you let your mind focus on something entirely different. Driving is like that."

"Hmm." Nell owned a nice enough car. She and the bank, anyway. If she needed to, she could squire people around from one address to another. At least until she got settled again in a new law firm. Cheyenne wasn't the largest city around, but Pastore Legal wasn't the only game in town.

She didn't have any idea how long that might take. She'd been working for Martin since she'd passed the bar. She had plenty of friends from other firms—mostly professional acquaintances if she were strictly honest—and she imagined that she'd be able to use that network to get some meetings sooner rather than later.

She hoped.

She wasn't a penniless college student anymore. She had savings. But between her student loans, her car and the rent on the condo she shared with Ros, that nest egg would quickly be consumed. "I'll keep it in mind," she told the driver. "Thanks."

The driver let her off shortly after and quickly drove away in her silent car, already on the way to her next fare.

Nell straightened her shoulders, blew out a deep breath and headed up the steps. She unlocked the door and went inside, automatically pushing the door closed firmly to make sure it latched, and listened.

The absolute silence told her that Ros wasn't there, and Nell's shoulders relaxed again.

She picked up the mail that was scattered on the floor from where it had been pushed through the mail slot in the door and left it and her purse on the narrow acrylic table behind the couch. The presence of the mail on the floor told her that Ros hadn't come home the night before, either.

It wasn't the first time. Unlike Nell, Ros *was* sleeping with the guy she'd been seeing for the past year. But none of the messages on Nell's phone was from her roommate, and Ros always let Nell know if she was staying out.

At least she had until their argument the afternoon before.

She scrubbed her hands down her face and carried her phone with her upstairs to her spacious room.

When she and Ros had rented the condo a few years earlier, they'd both been giddy with delight because one of the previous owners had combined two units into one, making for much larger digs. Both bedrooms were set up like master suites, with their own bathrooms. They shared a study that was lined with legal tomes on one side and the books that Nell's mother had collected while she'd been alive on the other. Both of them spent far more time in that room than they ever did in the gourmet kitchen that the unit also possessed.

The only time the kitchen was ever used for its intended purpose beyond rudimentary sandwiches or coffee was when Ros's boyfriend, Jonathan, was there to cook.

The only drawback was the lack of central air-conditioning, but A/C was needed only during the worst of summer anyway. More often than not, they spent their days at the well-cooled office and at night, window fans sufficed.

Because of the size, the rent was high, but between the two of them, they'd deemed it worth the financial stretch.

Now, Nell flipped on the shower to get it hot and plugged in her phone to charge the battery while she listened to all of the messages that had piled up overnight.

The first few were birthday wishes. But the tone of the messages began to change quickly enough from celebration to shock. Commiseration.

None of them, however, was from Ros.

Nell debated sending her a text, but set aside her phone instead. She brushed her teeth—twice—then showered until the hot water started to run cold.

Then, wrapped in a towel, she checked her phone again. Another half-dozen messages had arrived. Word was definitely getting around that she was out at Pastore Legal.

It was too depressing to respond to any of them so she turned off her phone altogether. Her head still pounded, but she felt somewhat more human. Mopping at her dripping hair with another towel, she went back downstairs and into the kitchen.

Coffee was the next order of business. And maybe some food. She had time on her hands now. She could buy a cookbook. Learn to make something besides a grilled cheese sandwich.

Her gaze fell on the plastic-wrapped loaf of bread.

He'd fixed her toast.

She snatched open the cupboard door to grab a coffee pod and shoved it into place, jabbing viciously at the button to start the brewer.

Had Archer heard the news yet?

She could just imagine what he'd have to say if he had.

"Should have taken me up on my offer," she muttered aloud as the coffee burbled out of the spout and into her bright yellow mug with *Lawyers have feelings too* printed on one side, *Allegedly* printed on the other. "Then you'd be partners in a multioffice firm instead of out on your behind."

She shook the thought out of her head. Nearly finished with law school, she'd believed it would be disastrous going into practice with Archer Templeton. Her allegiance had been to Martin Pastore. Becoming a junior associate there was her dream come true.

The coffee had barely stopped dripping when she yanked it out from beneath the spout. She followed the splash of cream she added with a chaser of sugar—the real stuff—and finally took a sip. It scorched her tongue, but in seconds she could feel the blessed caffeine hitting her system.

She aligned the loaf of bread neatly next to the side of the stainless steel refrigerator and carried her coffee out of the kitchen just in time to hear the rattle of the door lock.

Ros was home.

Nell's stomach churned. She tightened the knotted towel and perched on the narrow arm of the white leather couch.

A moment later, the door swung inward and Rosalind, who looked only slightly better than Nell felt, entered.

Her eyes skated over Nell. "You're here."

"I live here," she said quietly. "My leaving your father's firm doesn't change that."

Ros's lips thinned. She elbowed the door closed and tossed her keys into the stylized bowl sitting on the table next to Nell's purse. "Maybe it should."

Nell's breath left her in a puff. "*Ros*, come on."

"Why? You accused my father of collusion!" Rosalind spread her arms. "The very idea is so ridiculous it's pathetic."

Nell's fingers tightened around her coffee mug. "And as little as a week ago, I'd have agreed with you," she said quietly. "But I saw the records with my own eyes. While he was supposed to be acting on behalf of the court in a probate matter up in Weaver, he was taking money to influence the outcome of the case!" A whole lot of money, as it turned out.

"Well, the outcome *wasn't* influenced," Ros said flatly. "Instead of dying intestate like everyone thought, Otis Lambert *did* leave a will and when it came to light that was that. He left everything but his ranch on that mountain he owned to the state of Wyoming and instructed the ranch itself to be sold off. End of story."

"That doesn't erase what your father tried to do before the will was discovered! He was taking bribes, Ros!"

Her roommate's expression was set. "We're not going to agree about this, Nell. My father would never behave unethically. His reputation is impeccable."

Nell's hands were shaking. She set aside her coffee cup. "I didn't want to believe it, either. There's no way I'm mistaken." She was also badly afraid this instance hadn't been Martin's only transgression, despite his impeccable reputation. He'd been too blasé when she confronted him.

"He showed me the bank account, Nell. It's your name that is on it. Not his."

Nell swallowed hard. She was a lawyer. She knew better than to sign anything she hadn't read. But the amount of paperwork that flowed through

Martin's office was staggering. And she'd trusted him. A note left here or there for her to initial, to sign... She hadn't thought a thing about it. "He put it there."

Ros's expression turned pitying. "If this is about me making partner and you not—"

Nell stood. "This isn't about becoming a partner! For God's sake, Ros, you're my oldest friend. You're like a sister to me."

"And my father was like a father to you. Only he wasn't. You had your own, except he ran out on you when you were sixteen. And *my* father took you in!" Ros raked her fingers through her hair. It was just as dark as Nell's but where Nell's was uncontrollably curly, Ros's was thick and enviably straight. "*My* father who got you into law school. *My* father who hired you even though your grades were mediocre."

Nell's jaw tightened. Her grades might have been mediocre. But that didn't mean she wasn't good at her job now. She just hadn't been good enough, or she would have recognized what Martin had been up to earlier than she had. She would have never initialed this or signed that.

And Rosalind could talk until she was blue in the face about Martin's paternal devotion, but it had always come at a cost. He'd never been the loving father type. If Ros wanted his affection, she'd had to earn it by being a perfect reflection of him.

"You should be thanking him that he's not reporting the situation." Ros was shaking with her anger. "He's still showing loyalty to you and that certainly wouldn't be the case if he *hadn't* been like a father to you." She looked at the diamond watch around her wrist. "I think it's time you move out," she said abruptly.

"What? Right this minute?"

"Obviously not," she snapped and dropped her arm. "I've been thinking about this for a while."

That stung. "Since when?"

Her friend avoided her eyes. "Since a while now," Ros said defensively. "We're not college kids. We're too old to want or need a roommate. It's, well, it's embarrassing frankly."

That *really* stung. "And if I don't want to move? The lease is in both of our names."

"Then I'll move." Ros crossed her arms. "Jonathan and I have been talking about taking things to the next level. He wants a family and—"

Nell's eyebrows climbed into her hairline. "Do *you*? With Jonathan? Two months ago, you told me he was good in the kitchen, but outside of it, not so much!"

Ros looked annoyed at the reminder. "Even if you hadn't done what you did—"

"What *I* did?" Nell's voice rose even more.

"Rosalind Pastore, when have you *ever* known me to lie about something?"

Ros plowed onward. "It still would be time for us to start acting like the grown women that we are. I'm a partner at Pastore Legal now. I should—"

Nell lifted her hand, steeling herself. "Don't. I don't even want to hear it. Your father wants me out at the firm. You want me out of here. You always said you wanted to be like him, and you've succeeded. Congratulations." Her voice went a little hoarse and she picked up her coffee, struggling for composure. "Soon as I can arrange it, I'll be out of your hair, too."

Ros's eyes finally flickered, showing at least some semblance of emotion. "This didn't have to get this ugly, Nell."

She locked her knees. She felt like she'd been betrayed by everything she'd held dear for the last twenty years. She stared straight into her friend's eyes. Because she knew in her heart that she hadn't done one single thing wrong. Except put her faith where it didn't belong. "Didn't it?"

Ros was the first to look away. Then without another word, she ran quickly up the stairs. A moment later, Nell heard the slam of a bedroom door.

She sank down on the couch arm again, and covered her eyes with a shaking hand.

"You all right?"

Startled, she slipped right off the narrow edge of slick white leather to land ignominiously on the floor, hot coffee splashing everywhere. She grabbed the towel that had also slipped, barely keeping it above her breasts and below her butt, and stared at the door, which was slightly ajar.

Right at Archer's damned face peeking through the crack.

Chapter Three

Her cheeks burning more than her coffee-drenched thighs, Nell quickly righted herself so that she was on her knees. "Haven't you done enough? What are you doing here?"

He pushed the door open farther and stepped into the house. "I could hear your voices out on the street." He picked up the coffee mug, as it had continued rolling across the black-tiled floor right toward his feet.

"That doesn't give you permission to barge in."

He held out his hand. "Need help?"

"Not from you." With one hand keeping the bottom of the towel tucked against her thighs and the other keeping the top of it tucked against her chest, she managed to get to her feet. While she had only a length of coffee-splattered white terry cloth protecting her dignity, since earlier this morning, Archer had changed from the undershirt and navy pajama pants into blue jeans and a black pullover.

"And it wasn't closed, by the way."

She couldn't even argue the point with him, because the door often failed to latch the first time around. "If you're here to see your sister, she's upstairs."

He snorted and set the mug on the sofa table. "Stepsister. And no. I'm not."

"Then have you come here to gloat?"

"Because you've left Pastore Legal?"

She didn't understand why it disturbed her so much that he, more so than anyone else who'd been leaving her messages, knew about it. But it did.

"Nothing to gloat about," he said calmly, completely ignoring her stony silence. "I figure you're showing more sense than you have in the last ten, fifteen years." He angled his head, his gaze roving over her. "Did you burn your legs?"

She had, but what was the point of confirming it? "If I ask you to please, *please* leave, will you?"

His lips twitched. Her life felt like it was in the

toilet, but the man's infernal green eyes still had the nerve to sparkle. "What do you think?"

She let out an impatient sound and turned to make her own run up the stairs. Ros's bedroom door was tellingly shut as she passed it heading for her room on the opposite side of the hall.

She shut her door and went into her bathroom again, wetting a fresh cloth to wipe away the coffee on her legs. The skin was red and tender when she blotted it dry. Rather than dress in jeans, she pulled on a calf-length T-shirt dress that she usually wore only to sleep in.

As her hair was drying, it had begun twisting into its usual corkscrew curls and now she yanked it up and into a careless knot. Her reflection in the mirror looked a little feverish, but there wasn't anything she could do about it, so she went back downstairs.

Archer was sprawled on the unforgivingly hard, straight-backed couch as comfortably as he'd been sprawled on the overstuffed chair in his own home.

The coffee had also been wiped up from the floor, though there was a small wet spot on the edge of the area rug. It could have been a lot worse. The rug was as white as the couch.

"Just sit down, Nell," he said calmly when she hovered there at the base of the stairs. "And tell me what happened with Pastore."

Her hand tightened over the newel post. "After you tell *me* what happened last night." Her cheeks felt as feverish as they'd looked in her mirror.

"You mean after you were finished dancing on the bar?"

She winced. "I had hoped that was just a bad dream."

"Look at the bright side. At least you still had on your shirt when the cops showed."

She released the post and slunk over to the opposite end of the couch. The side chair that matched it was piled with law books that she kept meaning to take to the office. "Guess it's good I've already parted ways with Martin. If he heard about that, I'd have been in a different heap of trouble."

"Why *did* you part ways?"

She pressed her tongue against her teeth, studying his unfairly handsome face. "I didn't make partner." It was the truth; just not the truth he'd requested. "I thought it was time for a change."

His eyes narrowed, but after a moment, he shrugged slightly. "Okay. So now what? Have a plan?"

"I have a lot of contacts," she managed. "I'm sure I'll find a new firm without too much trouble."

"You can always work for me."

She couldn't stop the choked sound that rose

in her throat. "I know you don't mean that." And when he'd made the proposition of working together all those years ago, it had been a *with* situation, not a *for*.

He shrugged again. "It would sure piss off Ros, though. Which is par for the course. I'm already in the doghouse with one of my other sisters. Why not make it two."

She pressed her lips together and silence fell between them. She crossed her ankles, then uncrossed them. He showed no sign of leaving. And he still hadn't answered her question about what had occurred the night before.

She toyed with her ragged thumbnail and changed tack. "What doghouse with which sister?" Not including Rosalind, he had four, three of whom were identical triplets.

"Greer. Her youngest, Finn, turns one today. She and her husband, Ryder, are having a big party."

She gave him a sharp look. "Then why are you here?" He'd always put his family first. He was even loyal to Ros in a way. Despite the strained relationship Ros had with her mother, who lived several hours away in Braden, Archer made a point of personally delivering messages and the gifts that Meredith kept sending for birthdays and Christmases and every other little reason she could think of. Ros said he did it to annoy her. Nell had never been so sure. She would have loved to have a mother still around to send her messages and silly little gifts.

"I'll get over to Braden soon enough for cake," he told her.

Which reminded her of her own birthday cake from the day before. Birthday cake and champagne. Way too much champagne.

She folded her fingers together. "Why was I in your bed? We didn't, uh—"

"Play doctor like we used to?"

She gaped. "We never played doctor," she said in a fierce whisper.

He leaned across the cushion separating them. That faint, annoying smile played across his lips. He drew his finger slowly along her cheek, then tapped it once, lightly, against her lower lip.

Her skin burned and she found it very hard to breathe.

He leaned a few inches closer and his deep voice seemed to drop another octave into a whisper of his own. "Then how do we know what each other's bits and pieces look like?"

Every cell in her body lurched. "We agreed not to *ever* talk about that," she managed after a moment.

His smile widened slightly. "Times change. We didn't do anything wrong. As I recall, it was quite…right."

One night. One night during her last month of law school when she'd succumbed to his appeal.

Nell had never told anyone.

Not even Ros.

And it had taken her years before she'd managed to file the experience away in the dusty past where it belonged. While he had just continued onward, changing one woman on his arm for the next with routine ease.

The amazing thing was he'd never seemed to leave anyone with hard feelings.

Except her.

But admitting that then or now was anathema.

She stiffened her resolve. "You still haven't answered the question, either."

His lashes dropped slightly. He sat back, stretching out his long legs, and smiled his unreadable smile. "You were in my guest room," he finally said.

Relief swept through her. "Thank God."

He raised an eyebrow. "Don't need to sound so relieved there, Cornelia."

"Heaven forbid someone bruise your considerable ego." She pushed to her feet and stepped over his legs. "Your nephew's birthday party is waiting." She opened the door with a pointed flourish.

He exhaled as if she were the one trying his patience, and stood. He walked over to the door. "If you need me, you know how to reach me."

Her hand tightened around the doorknob. "I won't need you."

The amused tilt of his lips twisted slightly. "I know."

Then he stepped past her and strode down the walkway toward the fancy pickup truck parked at the curb.

She was still standing in the doorway watching when he drove away.

No. She wouldn't need him.

She wouldn't need anyone.

It was a lesson she'd learned when she'd been sixteen. And every time she'd forgotten it since then, all she'd earned was pain.

"I'm sorry, Nell." The director of the legal aid agency smiled apologetically. "I appreciate your offer, but we just don't have space for you."

Nell kept her own smile in place with an effort. It had been nearly six weeks since she'd left Pastore Legal. She'd put in her name at every firm in Cheyenne—whether they had openings or not. But now, to have her services—her *volunteer* services no less—turned down was the last straw.

"Sally." She met the director's eyes. "We've known each other for years. We have lunch at least once a month. Since when have you ever turned down a capable volunteer?"

Sally looked pained. She looked beyond Nell's

shoulder toward the open office area beyond. Then she folded her hands together and leaned forward over her untidy metal desk, her voice lowering confidentially. "I can't afford to get on the wrong side of Martin Pastore, Nell. You know how much pro bono his firm does for us."

Nell's fists curled. "What's he been saying?"

Sally lifted her shoulders, looking helpless. "Nothing actionable. But there are rumors about, well, I'm sorry, but about your overall competency. Things falling through the cracks that other people have had to cover for. Little things that add up to larger problems."

Nell's nerves tightened. After two weeks of failing to gain so much as a single interview, she'd begun wondering if Martin was manipulating things behind the scenes. She'd told herself she was being paranoid. But then a third week passed. And a fourth.

Ros had already managed to break the lease on their condo and move out. She'd been staying with Jonathan for weeks now. Which had left Nell on the hook for that month's rent on the oversize condo. She'd put in notice that she'd be vacating it in eleven days, even though she hadn't secured a replacement just yet. There were places she could rent. Just not ones that wanted an unemployed lawyer whose name was apparently mud.

"You know me better than that, Sally."

"I do, but… *Ros* made partner at Pastore."

"She's Martin's daughter," Nell reminded her stiffly.

"So did Scott Muelhaupt." Sally looked genuinely baffled. "He's new with the firm. You'd been there for years." She shook her head again. "I'm sorry. I wish I could do more for you, Nell. You know I like you, but—"

"But your agency likes Martin's firm more," Nell finished bluntly.

"Needs Martin's firm more," Sally corrected.

Nell exhaled. She stood. "I appreciate the honesty, Sally." At this point it was more than she'd received from anyone else.

"I'm sure things will work out in time." Sally followed her through the desks crowded into the office area toward the front door. "Once there's more distance from your departure from Pastore Legal."

Time was the one thing Nell didn't really have. Not that she intended to share that information with Sally Youngblood.

Once outside, she crossed to her car in the pitted parking lot and tossed her briefcase onto the passenger seat. Her back seat was filled with packing boxes. Same as her trunk. She'd rented a small storage unit and had been methodically transferring things there from the condo. These were the things she couldn't bear to part with—

like all of her mother's books—but that she didn't need for day-to-day living.

Even though she was loathe to part with any more cash than she had to, she needed coffee, particularly after that depressing meeting with Sally Youngblood. She drove to the coffeehouse on the corner of the next block where she paid for an exorbitant but delicious coffee before she proceeded to the storage facility.

Once she got there and parked, she couldn't find any of the carts that were supposed to always be available but weren't, so she carried the heavy boxes of books one after another to the unit. She'd chosen one on the second floor because it was cheaper. Unfortunately, the elevator was as readily available as the elusive carts and she always ended up having to use the stairs.

She figured it made up a little for the fact that she'd canceled her gym membership in order to save that monthly fee, too.

With her back seat and trunk empty once more, Nell sat in her car with the windows open because of the heat of the day and finished her coffee.

She'd lived in Cheyenne all her life and had never seriously contemplated relocating elsewhere. But how could she stay in Cheyenne and make a living considering the long reach of Martin Pastore?

She needed either a new location or a new

profession. Cheyenne was only a few hours from Denver. The city was huge compared with Cheyenne. But the rents were proportionately higher, as well. She was trying to make ends meet, not move those ends even further apart.

Which was the lesser evil?

No closer to an answer, she drove back to the condo. She couldn't even think of it as "home" anymore. Not with more than half of the furnishings gone after Ros had taken them. Not with Ros herself gone.

Despite everything, Nell couldn't help feeling the sharp, painful edge of her absence.

They'd been friends since elementary school. When Nell's mother had died when she'd been fourteen, Ros had cried with her. When Nell's father had run out on her just two years later, Ros had talked Martin into letting her live with them.

Nell's stomach churned. Stress had been taking its toll. Adding coffee on top of it had probably not been the wisest decision in the world.

Vowing to drink more water and less coffee, she went inside. She left the front door open as well as the windows in the kitchen in the back to encourage a cross breeze through the unit. The month of August was never very pleasant, but was even less so without central air-conditioning.

She made herself a tall glass of ice water, then went upstairs to the study.

It was nearly empty now, save the built-in desk where Nell's laptop sat looking forlorn, and one last shelf with a smattering of books. They were all first-edition children's books penned by her mother.

Julia Brewster had owned a bookstore. It had been small. Not hugely successful. And the first books she'd placed on her shelves had been the twelve books she'd written about a curious penguin named Monty. In fact, the first title had been just that. *Monty the Curious Penguin.*

Nell could still remember the vaguely dusty smell of the books as well as her horror when her father had sold the store and most of its contents lock, stock and barrel only months after her mother died.

Nell had spent years tracking down the Monty books. She had recovered them all except one. The tenth. *Monty Meets Mary.* In the eleventh book, Monty and Mary get married. And in the last book of the series, they have twin baby penguins.

Nell trailed her fingers along the colorful dust jackets, pausing between volumes nine and eleven. The books had been mildly successful for the two years when they'd been published thirty years ago. But there had been only the one printing and the publisher had gone out of business when Nell was still a teenager.

She'd finally had to give up on ever finding a copy of *Monty Meets Mary*.

Shaking off her melancholy, she placed the books in an empty box that she'd picked up at the grocery store. It smelled vaguely of the apples that it had originally contained, but that was better than bananas. And Nell had no room to be picky. With the books packed, she tucked in a few winter sweaters that she didn't figure she'd need in the next month, and carried the box downstairs.

She was just in time to meet the mail carrier, who seemed consternated over Nell's open door—it meant he couldn't push the postal items through the mail slot. She leafed through the small stack he'd finally put in her hands. Circulars and bills.

Sighing, she tossed them onto the side chair. It was the only piece of furniture left in the living room after Ros had taken her stuff.

Until the room was nearly empty, Nell hadn't put much thought into the fact that her roommate had chosen and paid for nearly everything on the first floor of the condo. Ros had liked a particular style and could afford to get what she'd wanted and Nell had never had a reason to argue with her.

She didn't even own a television. Not that she really needed one. A person could get all the news they wanted on their phones these days and Nell had always been more of a reader than a viewer.

With a legal pad and a pencil in hand, she took

her glass of water and went out the back door to sit on the step. She drew a line down the center of the page. She wrote *Stay* at the top on one side of the line and *Go* on the other.

Then she began to enumerate every point she could think of on each side of the decision.

Unfortunately, the exercise didn't garner any information she hadn't already thought of. She tossed the yellow pad of paper onto the cement step beside her and propped her elbows on her knees.

"You look like you're still fourteen years old."

She jerked, turned around and looked up to see Archer standing on the threshold of the back door. Apparently he'd just waltzed right through the apartment, meaning he'd been in her condo twice now in the span of six weeks. It was a record. And she was far less shocked to see him than she ought to have been.

"What are you doing here?"

He held up a package wrapped with brown craft paper and twine. "A care package from Meredith for Ros. But considering the lack of furniture in there, I'm assuming she's moved. Naturally, she wouldn't bother informing us about it. So I don't know where to take it."

"Could take it to her office," she pointed out waspishly.

"Yes, but then I'll have to breathe the same air

as her father, and I've already suffered that experience more than once this year. You know, anyone and their mother's brother could walk in through your open front door."

"Anyone *did*."

He leaned over and picked up her glass of water, then sat down on the step beside her.

She gave him a frowning look. "Seriously. What do you *want*?"

A hint of annoyance clouded his perpetually amused expression. "Seriously, maybe I don't *want* anything. That so hard to believe?"

"You are one of the busiest attorneys in the state." And how he managed it with only a few employees based in Denver totally escaped her. "You probably bill by the half second."

His lips twitched. "Every other minute."

She rolled her eyes, then reached past him. "Give me the pad."

He handed it to her.

She flipped to the next page and quickly wrote out Ros's new address. Then she tore off the page and extended it toward him. "She's living with Jonathan these days."

Archer glanced at the address, then folded it into a square that he pushed in his back pocket. His shoulder brushed against her when he did so and she tried hard not to react.

"How's the job hunting?"

She shrugged and was glad that her Stay/Go list was flipped over and away from his too-observant eyes. "Haven't found the right fit just yet."

He sipped her water as if he had every right to do so. "What really happened between you and Pastore?"

"I told you."

"You said you didn't make partner. That doesn't explain why he's been dropping little nuggets here and there about your professional fitness."

Her face burned. "Maybe I'm not fit." She hadn't yet reported Martin's actions on the Lambert estate to the bar association, and it should have been the first thing she did. But Ros had been right about one thing. Lambert's wishes with regard to his estate had been ultimately fulfilled regardless of the money Martin had accepted to manipulate the probate.

"Don't be stupid." For the first time, Archer looked and sounded impatient. "You're a good lawyer. Better than Pastore deserved, for damn sure."

Her eyes suddenly burned and she quickly looked away before he could see.

He shifted again, broad shoulder once more pushing against her while he reached into his pocket, this time extracting something. He held it out to her.

"What's that?" Though it was perfectly obvious what it was: an ivory-colored business card containing a single telephone number and nothing else.

"That's my grandmother's number. Vivian Archer Templeton. She lives in Weaver."

Nell eyed him, not sure where he was going with this. Weaver was as far away as his hometown of Braden. And both municipalities put together were still smaller than a quarter of Cheyenne. "So?"

He nudged the card toward her again. "She's looking for someone to head up her latest pet project."

"I don't need your pity any more than I needed your so-called offer to work for you."

He let out a short laugh. "Trust me. You wouldn't have gotten it working for me and you definitely won't get it working for Vivian. She's rich and eccentric. Which makes her a force that can only be understood through experience. My cousin Delia would attest to that. She's Vivian's personal assistant when she's not off gallivanting around doing something else like she is right now."

Nell still didn't take the card but she couldn't keep herself from being curious. "What's the project?"

"She wants to get a new public library built in

Weaver. Raising money, finding the property, getting it through the red tape. All of it."

She'd been there numerous times because of the Lambert estate. It had never even crossed her mind to think it would be a great place to live. "I'd have to go to Weaver."

He gave her a look. "And that's a negative? What've you got going here that's better?"

"I'd have to find a place to live there, too."

"Vivian's got a big house. If she takes a shine to you, she's got space for you to stay right there. And if that's too close for comfort for you, you can use the guesthouse out at my place," he added, sounding casual. "I'm never there and you can feed my cat."

"You don't have a cat." Then she frowned at him. "Do you?"

His lips twitched. "What do you think?"

She exhaled and rolled her eyes again.

"Look, I don't care where you live. I'm just saying there are options for you."

She wasn't really going to consider it, was she? She slowly slid the card from his fingers, carefully avoiding touching him. "I'll think about it."

"Don't think too long. Vivian's not a young woman. She needs help on the project sooner rather than later. If you don't step up, someone else will. If you were working for her, it'd give you time to regroup. Figure out what it is you really want to do."

"I'm a lawyer. That's what I really want to do." She narrowed her eyes at him. "What's that look for?"

He spread his hands innocently. "What look? You going to call her or not?"

"I said I'll think about it."

"Right." He suddenly stretched out his legs and stood, then picked up the twine-wrapped package. "Let me know if you need me."

"I won't need you," she replied by rote.

"I know." He lightly knuckled her head as if she were a little kid, then went into the kitchen. She could hear him whistling softly as he left.

Nell picked up the yellow pad and looked at her Stay/Go list.

On the Go side, she penciled in one word.

Archer.

Then she sighed faintly and tossed aside the pad.

Chapter Four

Vivian Templeton turned out to be a diminutive woman well into her eighties. She had perfectly coiffed silver hair and diamond rings on every finger, and lived in a mansion—an honest-to-goodness mansion—located on the edge of Weaver.

Thanks to all of the work that Nell had done on the Lambert estate and the Rambling Mountain matter, she was fairly well versed with the Weaver demographics. In a region populated by more cows than people, as a general rule, mansions weren't the norm. As often as not, a person's barn was bigger than their abode.

She'd been hard-pressed not to stand there with her mouth hanging open when she'd arrived for the meeting that she'd arranged with Archer's grandmother. She'd been met at the door by a bald guy wearing an ivory ascot and formal black suit who'd introduced himself as Montrose before leading her through to a two-story atrium.

Vivian's office was on the second floor. It had windows that overlooked the rear of her property and Rambling Mountain loomed violet and gray in the distance.

Nell had never stepped foot on the mountain—it had been privately owned land until Otis Lambert died. She wondered if Archer had.

She pushed the thought of him out of her mind and focused harder on the petite woman across from her.

"The biggest challenge," Vivian was saying now, "is the town council. One of the members in particular who is unreasonably opposed to anything I try to accomplish in this town." Her lips thinned. "But not even people like Squire Clay can stop progress when it's warranted, and a library properly sized and outfitted for a growing community is certainly warranted." She looked over the top edge of her reading glasses at Nell. "Do you read, my dear?"

Feeling bemused, Nell nodded. "My mother owned a small bookstore, actually."

"A businesswoman." Vivian nodded approvingly. "Has she given it up?"

Nell shook her head. "She died when I was fourteen. My father sold the business shortly after."

That earned another look over the edge of the glasses. "I'm sorry."

Nell assumed Vivian was sorry about her mother versus the business, but she wasn't entirely certain. "Thank you," she said, which seemed to cover her bases either way.

Vivian was giving Nell a close look as she toyed with the heavy strands of pearls hanging around her fragile-looking neck. Her demeanor told Nell she was already moving on. "Archer speaks highly of you."

She was grateful that her cheeks didn't get too hot. "I'm not sure why," she admitted. "More often than not we've been on opposing sides in the courtroom."

"Respecting a worthy opponent is as valuable as respecting one's close associates." Vivian took off her glasses and dropped them atop the résumé that Nell had brought with her. A résumé that Vivian had completely ignored. "I'm afraid the position doesn't pay as much as you must be used to getting."

She proceeded to name a figure that Nell had

a hard time not choking over. Not because it was so low. But because it was so high.

Whatever Vivian Templeton was used to paying her lawyers, it bore no resemblance to what Martin had paid his associates.

"If that's acceptable—" Vivian's expression was confident, and at that high a salary, why wouldn't it be? "—when would you be able to start?"

Nell hid the relief bubbling inside her and glanced at her résumé. "Any time, really," she said calmly. "Once you've had an opportunity to review my references—"

Vivian waved a dismissive hand and sunlight caught in the diamonds on her fingers, dancing across the mild look of distaste on her face. "My grandson is the only reference I need," she assured. "I trust his judgment."

If the woman knew, or cared, about the rumors Martin had been circulating regarding Nell, she didn't show it.

Vivian folded her hands together. "So, that leaves the metaphorical ball in your court, dear. Would you like the position? I can't promise you a nine-to-five—frankly the thought of that makes me shudder. Dreary, don't you think?" She didn't wait for a response. "But I can promise you an interesting variety of tasks. If you like to be busy—"

"I do," Nell said quickly.

Vivian looked pleased. "Excellent. Is next Monday agreeable?"

It was already Thursday. That would leave Nell with a very busy few days before Monday, but she nodded with more confidence than she felt. "Perfectly agreeable." She'd been preparing to move out of the condo anyway. What difference did it make if she did it over this weekend or the next?

"Will you need assistance getting settled here in Weaver?"

Nell prided herself on her independence, and the last several weeks had already given her a blow in that arena. The last thing she wanted was for her new employer to think she couldn't handle such basic matters. "I have it covered, thank you." She didn't, but she would.

Again, Vivian smiled as if pleased. "When Archer called me this morning, he told me again just how eminently capable you are. He mentioned you've known one another since law school. As many lawyers as I've needed in my life, perhaps I should have gone to law school myself. Would have saved a fortune in retainer fees. Obviously you weren't Archer's type, but you were good friends with Meredith's daughter, Rosalind, is that correct?"

Were. Vivian couldn't know how correct she really was. But Nell highly doubted that Archer would have bothered sharing the details of her fractured friendship with his stepsister. "Ros recently moved in with her boyfriend, but up until then, we'd been roommates since school." The facts were accurate, despite the real cause behind Ros's actions. And Nell wasn't touching Vivian's blunt comment about not being Archer's type. "Your grandson was in his last year when she and I were in our first."

"I've met Rosalind," Vivian said. "Takes after my son's wife in looks. Quite beautiful. I never trusted beautiful female attorneys." She looked at Nell and nodded with satisfaction. "Welcome aboard."

Nell managed not to wince. Vivian obviously didn't consider *her* a beautiful female attorney.

Her new employer stood and tugged lightly at the three-quarter-length sleeves of her nubby pink suit. Nell didn't have a lot of personal experience with high-end designer clothes, but she was willing to bet that the suit carried a very fancy label.

She'd learned enough about Vivian Archer Templeton to know that she hailed from Pennsylvania and that most of her money came from her first husband—Archer's grandfather—who'd been in the steel industry. The several husbands who'd followed had only added to her wealth.

As a result, Nell doubted that Vivian had ever had to worry about retainer fees stretching her beyond her means.

She stood too and stuck out her hand. "I appreciate your confidence. I'm looking forward to proving it isn't misplaced."

Considering her overall air of delicacy, Vivian's handshake was surprisingly firm. Then she led the way out of the office, lightly clasping the filigreed balustrade that overlooked the rest of the atrium below. She went as far as the curving staircase where Montrose was waiting, as if he had some magical sixth sense that the meeting between Vivian and Nell had concluded.

"Montrose will see you out," Vivian told Nell. "He can give you the tour on Monday when you arrive. He also can answer any questions you might have before then. One of my granddaughters has been acting as my personal assistant, but she's away right now. So my man is delighted to fill in for Delia." Vivian smiled at Montrose, and Nell was certain that she saw a hint of deviltry in her eyes.

The same kind of deviltry that often lurked in Archer's eyes.

As for Montrose, he was clearly *not* delighted to be doing any such thing but he managed to exude both boredom and superiority.

Under other circumstances, Nell would have been hard-pressed not to giggle. She felt a little as if she'd landed in some alternate universe.

Instead, she kept her composure firmly in place

and followed Montrose's sedate descent down the fancy, curving staircase. It had a twin staircase on the other side of the room. Both led up to the second-floor landing that circled the entire space. "Are you in charge of the plants, Mr. Montrose? I've never seen anything so incredible."

The windows looked out on the wilds of Wyoming, but inside, a person would think they'd landed in a rain forest. The atrium was filled with exotic plants.

Just one more reason why it all felt a bit unreal.

"It is just *Montrose*," he was saying with the faintest of sneers. "And I'm Mrs. Templeton's *chef*."

For a moment she wished Ros could have heard him. He made Nell's Snape-ishness sound tame. "I certainly don't need to take you away from your usual duties. I'm sure I can find my way out if—"

He cut a glance her way that effectively silenced her, and she followed him down the rest of the stairs and through a few doors that disappeared seamlessly into the wall as they swung shut behind them.

Eventually, he reached the massive door through which she'd entered the mansion and held it open for her, bowing his head as she passed through. "I suppose you'll be moving into one of the guest rooms." His tone didn't change but it was clear as day that he didn't welcome the idea.

She was no more inclined to discuss her housing needs with him than she had been with his boss. "Not that I'm aware of," she said with her own measure of coolness. "It's not something that has been discussed."

"It will be. Since she's come to Wyoming, Mrs. Templeton has developed the habit of taking in strays."

"I'm not a stray," Nell said evenly. "I'll see you Monday morning, Montrose. Have a pleasant afternoon." Before he could say anything else, she turned and briskly crossed the courtyard paved in herringbone bricks to where she'd parked her car. Her nerves were jangling as she got behind the wheel and drove away from the mansion.

But she didn't give in to them until she was well away from the mansion.

Then she pulled off the side of the highway, put the car in Park and lowered her forehead to her steering wheel, hauling in several long, deep breaths. She had a job. She'd have money coming in again.

And even though the position with Mrs. Templeton was temporary, it would give Nell some needed breathing space until she could situate herself more permanently.

Regroup. Figure out what it really is you want to do.

Archer's words circled around inside her head

but then a livestock semi roared past, making her car rock slightly, and she sat up again. She blew out a cleansing breath.

"You're moving to Weaver," she said aloud. She absolutely was not going to entertain the notion of living at Vivian Templeton's mansion if that option even arose. And although Archer had tossed out the suggestion that she use his guesthouse, she couldn't imagine that he'd been serious.

She'd find a place to rent that didn't involve him.

She waited until the narrow highway was clear again, then pulled out and finished the short drive into the town proper. Because of her previous times there, she was already somewhat familiar with Weaver. She knew that the newer part of town was on the far side, toward Braden, which was the next closest town—some thirty miles away. She was now driving through the more historical center of town. The speed limit was cut in half as the highway turned into the main drag.

She drove past a picturesque park with a white gazebo in the middle of it, then the courthouse where she'd spent many hours sitting next to Martin Pastore as he administrated the Lambert estate on behalf of the state. And all that time she'd been oblivious to his under-the-table dealings.

She let out a frustrated grunt directed solely at herself. "Move *on*, Cornelia," she muttered as she slowed even further for a pickup truck reversing out of a slanted parking space into the street.

When the truck was finished, it drove ahead of her and she impetuously angled her car into the spot it had just vacated. When her front wheels bumped the curb slightly, she parked, grabbed her briefcase and climbed from the car. She automatically locked it, then crossed the sidewalk and entered the restaurant on the other side.

It was crowded. Lunch rush, Nell thought, and instead of joining the group of people standing to one side against the wall who were obviously waiting for tables, she crossed to the counter where one stool remained unoccupied near the cash register.

The older gentleman sitting on the stool next to it glanced at her when she set her briefcase on the floor.

"Mind if I sit here?" She touched her fingertips to the red vinyl-covered seat.

"Only if you mind sitting next to me," he said with a drawl. He had iron-gray hair, and the lines on his face could mean he was anywhere from sixty to eighty. His blue eyes were strikingly pale, sharp and clear, and held a glint of humor.

She smiled in return and slipped out of her suit jacket. She folded it and laid it over the top of her briefcase. "Busy place." She slid onto the round stool.

The man smiled. The humorous glint in his eye seemed to take on a new dimension. "That it is. Take it you haven't been to Ruby's before." His gaze flicked to her briefcase sitting on the floor between their seats.

She shook her head.

"You're in for a treat, then. Specials are there." He nodded toward the chalkboard on the wall. "I'm partial to the meat loaf sandwich." He glanced at the very young, dark-haired waitress who approached and set an insulated coffeepot in front of him. "Thank you, darlin'."

The woman had a friendly smile and a pencil stuck in her untidy ponytail. "Sounds like Squire's been telling you about the menu," she said, nodding at Nell in greeting.

Nell couldn't help her small start of surprise at the name. She figured he was likely the same Squire whom Vivian had mentioned. It wasn't exactly a common name.

"I'm Tina." The waitress was sliding a plastic-coated menu on the counter toward Nell. "Can I get you something to drink? Water? Soda pop?"

The man next to her—Squire—was loosening the lid on the urn filled with fragrant coffee.

She started to order coffee, too, but hesitated when she saw him pour his coffee into a nearly flat saucer rather than the cup itself. Then with the saucer balanced on his fingertips, he sipped from the edge.

She realized she was staring and looked quickly toward Tina. "Coffee," she finished, "with cream and sugar, please." None of the other diners seated at the counter seemed to even notice Squire's unorthodox use of his drinkware.

Tina set a cup and saucer on the counter, turned the cup upright and filled it from another pot of coffee that she pulled from the warmer on the giant machine behind the counter. With her free hand, she set a small pitcher containing real cream on the counter, then added a tall glass sugar dispenser with a metal cap. "Specials are on the board," she said, reiterating what Nell's counter mate had already pointed out. "We're out of cherry pie, though."

"Order up!" A grizzled man's face briefly appeared in the pass-through window to the kitchen. A thick white plate full of food clattered slightly when he set it on the stainless steel ledge. Then his face disappeared from view again.

Tina turned away from Nell and grabbed the plate. "Thanks, Bubba," she called through the pass-through before delivering it to a patron at the far end of the counter. On her way back, she scooped up a check and a wad of cash and coins.

There was music playing—presumably from the shining jukebox standing in one corner. It wasn't loud enough to rise above the clatter of dishes and voices, though. Half the occupants of the diner were men; nearly all possessed hat marks in their hair from the cowboy hats and ball caps that sat on tables or the ledges on the backs of booths. Three women still wore their cowboy hats and one had a mass of dreads piled to a spectacular height atop her head.

The cash register pinged softly as Tina deposited the money, then she turned to Nell once again and pulled her pencil from her ponytail. "What can I get you?"

The slab of meat loaf between thick slices of bread on Squire's plate did look appetizing, but the scent of grilling burgers reigned supreme for Nell. Even though she hadn't really looked at the menu and it wasn't listed on the chalkboard, Nell ordered a cheeseburger and fries.

"You bet." Tina turned away again and stuck the order she'd written on the revolving rack in the pass-through. She turned back again with almost balletic grace and looked at the man next to Nell. "Squire, anything else I can get for you? Slice of chocolate pie?"

The man shook his head. "Think I'll pass, darlin'. All these weeks o' this fine food and my shirts are getting tight." He patted the front of his faded blue chambray shirt.

Nell glanced at him. His stomach looked flatter than her own. Regardless of his age, he also looked fitter than her, too. "You eat here often, then?"

"Every day since I've worked here," Tina answered before Squire could. She set a napkin and flatware in place for Nell. "Nearly four months now." She winked at Squire. "My boyfriend's completely jealous, too, of my lunchtime date."

Squire chuckled, though the sound of it seemed a little forced to Nell.

Another waitress—this one older than Tina—stopped at the cash register and stuck a check on the spindle. She gave Squire a stern look that was belied by the smile on her face. "You promised you'd stop flirting with my servers, Squire. What am I going to do with you?"

"As much as I love you, Tabby girl, I'm too old to change my ways now. That grandson of mine you married should have told you that by now."

Tabby's eyes sparkled. When she rounded the counter again, she dropped a fond kiss on Squire's tanned, weathered cheek, greeted another customer by name as he entered, and headed off.

Nell didn't know if Tabby managed or owned the restaurant, but given the comment about her servers, she figured it was one or the other. It dawned on her, then, that the look in Squire's eyes earlier had been pride.

Vivian wore a similar expression whenever she spoke of Archer.

Nell looked at her counter mate. "Something tells me you know a lot about this town." She extended her hand. If this man actually was Vivian's roadblock on the town council, she might as well get off on a good footing with him while she had a chance to. "I'm Nell Brewster. I'm moving here from Cheyenne."

His eyes crinkled as he returned the handshake. "Squire Clay," he offered, thus confirming Nell's assumption. "And you've made a fine choice. I'll take Weaver any day over Cheyenne." He slanted a look toward her briefcase. "Not many folks carry one of those around these parts."

She lifted her shoulder. "Professional habit, I'm afraid," she admitted wryly. "Lawyer by trade."

His eyes narrowed slightly as he studied her face. "You coming on with Tom Hook? Heard he was looking for someone."

"No." She didn't even know who Tom Hook was. "Not planning to officially practice here." Not yet, at any rate. She unfolded the large paper napkin over her lap as Tina set a basket heaped with glistening golden fries and a plate with her cheeseburger and fixings in front of her. "Thanks, Tina."

"Ketchup and mustard?"

"Just the mustard." She took the bottle when it

quickly appeared and squirted out a dollop on her burger. She arranged the lettuce and sliced tomato on top of that, fit the bun in place and decided she was never going to be able to get her mouth around the thing. She picked up her knife. "I have the feeling that you know everything about this town, Mr. Clay," she told Squire as she cut her burger in half. "Can you give me the skinny on where I should begin looking for a place to rent? I don't have the luxury of a lot of time."

"Make it Squire, child," he said immediately. "Lot of apartments out by Shop-World. If that's your cup of tea."

"Whatever is affordable and safe is my cup of tea right now," she admitted wryly. She took a bite of the hamburger and nearly groaned in pleasure.

"Ain't a thing Bubba Bumble can't cook," Squire said with a knowing nod.

She dabbed her napkin at her chin and sent a chaser of French fry after the burger. It was salty. Perfectly crisp on the outside. Tender and airily light on the inside. "Oh...my," she said once she swallowed. She eyed the man next to her. "No wonder you come here every day."

He chuckled but the humor in his eyes seemed dimmed. "Things become a habit when you never expect it." He looked over his shoulder. "Tabby," he called out, "you have any vacancies at your triplex?"

The waitress, delivering a tray of food to a table of three women and six children, paused. "Not right now." When the delay in service earned her a cacophony of whiny complaints, she quickly turned her attention back to her customers and began doling out the baskets of food to the children. "Check the bulletin board," she suggested. "People tack up all sorts of notices."

Squire glanced at Nell again. "By the door. You passed it on your way in." He dropped his napkin atop his unfinished sandwich. "Most of the people who come in here are locals. You won't go wrong with anything posted here." He dropped some cash on the counter and stood. He was taller than Nell expected. "But if you have a question 'bout anything, come back here for lunch again tomorrow. I'll be here." He gave her a faint wink and then strode toward the door, offering a few comments to other patrons as he departed.

Nell turned her attention back to her meal and watched as Tina cleared away Squire's plate. The only thing he'd finished was the coffee. "He's really here every day?"

"Seven days a week," Tina confirmed. She filled another insulated carafe and left it for Nell. "You doing all right?"

"Yes, thanks." Since it didn't seem as though anyone was in a rush to claim Squire's vacated seat, she moved her jacket to it and flipped open the top of her briefcase. It was an old-fashioned sort of thing but it was sturdy enough to cart around the mountain of legal files and briefs that she no longer needed to tote around. She pulled out her cell phone and flipped the case closed again and then caught Tina's attention. "Don't clear this away. I'll be right back."

The busy waitress nodded and Nell went over to the front door and quickly scanned the bulletin board that was no longer blocked by waiting patrons. There were only two for-rent notices, though. She snapped photos of both, then turned back to return to the counter, but the sight of the tall blond man striding along the sidewalk outside the windows stopped her.

She had the silliest desire to duck and hide, but it was almost as if Archer knew it, because his head turned and his eyes met hers. A moment later, he'd reached the door and was pushing through it.

His eyes were devilish. "As I live and breathe. It's Cornelia Brewster."

She gave him a look and returned to the counter and her meal. He slid onto the seat that Squire had vacated. There was just as much space between the two seats as there had been before, but now it felt like it had been cut in half.

She angled her shoulder as far away as she

could to keep it from brushing against him. "I'll never believe it's a coincidence that you're here."

"Why not? The world revolves on coincidences."

"You've talked with your grandmother."

"Nope. I was, however, meeting with a client over at the jailhouse. And anyone who knows anything knows that when you're in Weaver and you have a chance to eat at Ruby's, you don't pass it up." Looking as if he had frequently not passed it up, he reached right over the counter and retrieved a clean mug from the rack stored below. Then he filled it from the coffeepot that Tina had left for Nell.

She thought about protesting, but concentrated instead on the excellent food. And she couldn't really complain since he topped off her own cup at the same time.

"Unless you're checking out other opportunities of employment here," he said after he tightened the lid on the urn again, "I'll assume that *you* have talked with her."

"Yes." She almost didn't want to tell him, because he'd probably just crow about it. But then again, if it weren't for him, she'd have never met with Vivian in the first place. Which meant he had more of a right to crow than she did to feel churlish. "I start on Monday."

He didn't look surprised at all. His arm brushed

hers as he lifted his coffee mug in a toast. "Congratulations."

She managed a smile and shoved two French fries in her mouth because she felt oddly shaky all of a sudden.

"Need help moving?"

More fries went into her mouth as she shook her head emphatically.

"And you wouldn't admit it if you did."

She wasn't going to deny it. She toyed with her coffee cup. "Thank you for putting in a good word for me," she finally said once her mouth was French fry–free. "I owe you."

His shoulder bumped hers, this time quite deliberately. "Almost kills you to say that, doesn't it."

She wasn't going to deny that, either.

He knew it, too, judging by the soft laugh he gave.

He waved at the second half of her cheeseburger. "You going to eat that?"

"Yes." She covered it protectively with her hand. "So don't think you're going to have it." That's what he'd always done back in law school, too. Finished whatever food was left alone for a moment. He'd always been ravenous and she'd never quite understood where he put it, since there had never been an ounce of extra weight on his broad-shouldered frame.

"Just making sure you are," he said blithely. "You're very thin."

It wasn't a compliment.

Tina returned. "Hi, Archer." She leaned her hip against the counter and smiled in a way that made Nell wonder just how serious the girl and the supposedly jealous boyfriend actually were. "What can I get for you?"

"Just the coffee."

"You sure?" Tina's cheeks turned a rosy pink despite her bold tone. "I've got a lot more to offer."

His chuckle was just the right amount of rueful not to cause offense. "One vice at a time, doll."

Tina sighed loudly and dramatically. "One of these days you're going to realize what you're missing."

He lifted his coffee cup. "No doubt."

She laughed and went off again to serve her other customers.

"She's way too young for you," Nell muttered from the side of her mouth.

"Calm your outraged sensibilities."

"I'm not outraged," she retorted. "But I imagine Judge Potts might have something to say about your flirtations."

"I doubt that, too." He folded his arms on the counter and leaned on them as he watched her. "I'm glad things are working out with Vivian."

"You could have warned me about her house, you know. It's a little more than just *big*."

"Ten bedrooms at last count. She's made some noises lately about adding another wing."

Nell nearly choked on her coffee. "For what?"

"Who knows?" His green eyes stayed focused on her face in a way that felt intensely intimate. "Vivian knows her own mind. I've seen what she can do with her money for others. I say if she wants to build another wing for herself, it's her business."

"Maybe it's a wing for Montrose."

Archer laughed outright. "He's a trip, isn't he?"

Nell couldn't keep from smiling, too. "That's one word for it."

"He's devoted to Vivian, though. And she to him, I'd have to say."

Nell lifted her eyebrows. "Are they—"

"God no," he said immediately, grimacing at the thought. "That's an idea that makes me want to wash out my brain. I take it she hasn't mentioned 'dear Arthur—'" he air-quoted the words "—to you, yet?"

She shook her head.

"He was her final husband and according to her, the most decent man to ever exist. And he was the greatest love of her life. Most of those good things she's done with her money since she's transplanted herself here have been because of the late, dear Arthur."

"How long ago did he die?"

"Quite a few years now. None of us ever met him. But he's a presence in Vivian's life regardless of how long he's been gone. She's still trying to live up to his standard."

"I don't know if that's romantic or sad."

Archer shifted and his arm brushed hers again.

Then she realized he'd pulled out his wallet and the cash he extracted and set on the counter was far too much for just a coffee.

She bristled. "I can afford to buy my own lunch."

"Actually, it's for the cat food."

"What?"

"The cat." He pushed the stack of bills closer to her. "Food," he repeated as if she were thick.

"We're back to that again?"

"He doesn't have a name. But he keeps coming around to eat and I'm going to be gone for the next several weeks on a case. Wouldn't want him to starve."

She didn't touch the money. "Why is it up to me to get him fed? You spend a lot of time in Cheyenne and Denver. More time than here, probably. What do you do then? Surely you have someone else who—"

"You just said it yourself. You owe me. And I

know you like cats because you told me so a long time ago."

She remembered the conversation very clearly. Because it had been the same day she'd ended up in his bed.

Not a guest room bed, either.

She shifted, trying to squelch the memory of bells ringing. Cymbals crashing. "My last experience taking care of a cat was more than twenty years ago." The cat she'd told him about. The one who had been her mother's. The one who'd disappeared after she died.

Only later, after her father had sold the bookstore, did Nell suspect the cat's exit had been his doing, too.

"It's not complicated," Archer said drily, completely ignoring her discouraging tone. "You pour some kibble in the bowl and the cat comes around and eats it."

"Don't you live out toward Braden?" She distinctly remembered Ros mentioning it once. She'd been highly annoyed because she'd needed to see him about something and it had necessitated the long drive.

"Yep." He tipped the coffeepot over his mug again, getting the very last few drops.

"I am *not* going to use your guesthouse," she warned adamantly. "If that's what you've got brewing in your mind." There was absolutely no logic to that offer, if he'd even been serious about it in the first place. She wouldn't be beholden to him, and he knew it.

"It's going to be a pain driving out there just to feed a cat, but that's up to you." He honestly sounded as if he didn't care.

She exhaled, impatient with herself for even allowing herself to get sucked into this. "There's really a cat?"

He gave her an innocent look that she didn't buy for a second. "Would I lie?"

Chapter Five

Nell eyed the empty pet food bowl.

She'd filled it with dry cat food the afternoon before, set it on top of the stone pillar where Archer had told her to set it, and now it was empty.

She looked at the pillar. It was about a foot across and at least six feet high. Taller than she was. Not so tall that a cat wouldn't be able to get up to it, though.

It was part of a gate marking the entrance to Archer's property. Archer said he never bothered to close the gate. He didn't keep any livestock on his ten acres of land. He just liked having the space around the house.

The house that Nell had chosen not to drive to. She didn't need to see it up close.

It was bad enough to know that the land where it was located was positively majestic in a stark sort of way. Scrubby brush grew in pale grayish-green shoots and sprigs of wildflowers clung around the bases of the boulders that dotted the relatively flat landscape.

It looked like a home for dinosaurs and snakes. Not for a stray cat.

Did birds eat cat food?

It seemed like a more plausible reason for the empty bowl.

Still feeling like she was playing in some silly game with Archer, she poured more food into the metal bowl and returned it to the top of the pillar.

It was her second day of working for Archer's grandmother. And her second day of driving nearly twenty miles out of town to feed his cat that may or may not actually exist.

She was an idiot. That's what she was.

She twisted the top of the cat food bag closed and returned it to the back seat of her car, then got behind the wheel and drove to Weaver. Twenty miles in a metropolitan area wasn't much of a big deal. Twenty miles on the very winding road running between Weaver and Braden, on the other hand, took a long time.

When she reached the Cozy Night motel, where

she'd been renting a room since Sunday night, it was nearly dark.

Inside the room, though, the lamp worked just fine. She dropped her purse on the nightstand between the two beds—one which was covered entirely with suitcases containing all of the clothes that she hadn't left in the storage unit in Cheyenne—and kicked off her shoes. It was warm and stuffy in the room after being closed up all day and after she changed out of her suit into a pair of shorts and a T-shirt, she opened the door again to let the air circulate.

It would cool off soon enough and she preferred fresh air rather than the rattling noise and forced chill provided by the air-conditioning unit that was located beneath the room's only window.

The Cozy Night wasn't fancy. But it was clean and it was affordable, even if she ended up having to stay there for a month. Which was how things were looking when it came to finding an actual rental.

The two listings on the board at Ruby's Diner hadn't panned out. Both had already been rented when she called. There were two apartment complexes on the other side of town, but they were both nearly full. The units available were either too large—and astonishingly, too expensive—or they weren't coming available until next month.

Nell still didn't believe she'd have difficulty

finding a place to live. Not in Weaver. But if she had to, she could continue staying at the Cozy Night for a while. It wasn't perfect. With only a dorm-sized refrigerator and a hot plate, it wasn't exactly equipped with kitchen facilities.

But then again, she hadn't exactly cooked back in Cheyenne, either.

She extracted a bottle of juice from the refrigerator and carried it with her outside the room.

There was an old-fashioned metal chair that had obviously been painted over a number of times—it was currently a not-unattractive shade of salmon—sitting outside the door of each room. Twenty-two chairs, stretching from one wing to the other. Depending on a person's viewpoint, it looked either stylishly retro, or completely out of date.

She sat in her chair with her legs outstretched and debated whether she could satisfy herself with a can of soup heated on the hot plate or if she needed to go farther afield. But having spent more than an hour driving back and forth to feed a possibly nonexistent cat with no name, going out again held little appeal.

"Can of soup it is," she murmured to herself.

But later.

For now, she relaxed in her chair—the metal bounced slightly if she shifted, sort of like a rocker—and sipped her juice.

The motel was situated on top of a small rise on the road before it dipped down again toward what she'd termed "Old Weaver."

"New Weaver" was the Shop-World region. Cee-Vid was located in New Weaver. It was a large gaming company owned by one of Weaver's longtime residents, Tristan Clay. She'd learned that from Vivian's nemesis, Squire, who had indeed been sitting on that same stool in Ruby's Diner that very afternoon. Tristan was Squire's youngest son. He'd also told her about his other four sons, who all lived in the area, too.

She'd run into the diner to grab a quick sandwich between errands for Vivian and he'd waved her over, patting the seat beside him.

There was something decidedly engaging about the old man, even though he was one of the roadblocks in the way of Vivian's library project. Something engaging but also something that struck Nell as a little sad. Maybe the fact that he talked about all of those sons, but still spent every afternoon having lunch in a diner?

But what could a person learn about another person over a half hour? Considering her debacle with Martin, she was having a hard time trusting her own sense of judgment.

From her salmon-colored perch, Nell watched lights begin to flicker. There were a lot more clustered together on the New Weaver side. The population of residents on that side of town was denser. Younger. They were the employees at Cee-Vid. At Shop-World. At the dozens of other small businesses that inevitably cropped up in everyday towns to support the growing needs of those citizens as they settled. Got married. Bought houses and had babies.

An old, rusting car turned into the motel parking lot. Its headlights washed over Nell before it came to a stop in front of the unit next to hers. Even before the engine cut out, the back doors opened and three ginger-haired kids tumbled out.

They spotted her and waved, but their steps didn't really slow as they raced around the car toward the small, fenced swimming pool that the Cozy Night offered its guests.

George, Blake and Vince.

She'd met the boys on Sunday when their mom, Gardner, who was obviously an avid country music fan, had ordered them to help their new "neighbor" carry her suitcases in from her car.

Gardner and her boys had been living at the Cozy Night for most of the summer now. Which was one of the reasons why Nell figured she could hack it for a while there, too, if it came to that.

"Need any help?" she called to the young mother as she opened her trunk.

Gardner shook her head. "I don't have much, Nell. Thanks, though." She ducked momentarily below the opened trunk, then straightened and slammed it shut. When she rounded the vehicle, she was carrying a single paper bag bulging with groceries. In addition to the dorm-sized fridge, Gardner's unit next door possessed a double-sided hot plate and a microwave. "How'd your day go?" she asked as she unlocked the door of the unit next to Nell's.

"Good. Yours?" Gardner was a hairdresser by trade but was currently making her motel rent by working at an ice cream shop in New Weaver.

The other woman hadn't explained more than that when they'd met on Sunday. And Nell hadn't explained any more about her own situation.

"Not bad," Gardner said as she pushed open the door to her room. "This heat has a lot of people in the mood for ice cream, so that's the good thing. I'll be out in a second. Want a cold drink?"

Nell lifted her juice. "I'm fine. Thanks."

The other woman disappeared and emerged a few minutes later. She'd exchanged her "Udder Huddle" T-shirt and jeans for a plain blue one-piece swimsuit. She had a striped towel draped around her neck, but instead of following her boys to the pool, she threw herself down into her own salmon-colored chair and popped the top on a can of soda.

From the pool area, they could hear the whoops and splashes from the boys.

Gardner exhaled and stretched out her legs far enough that she could prop the toe of her sandal on the bumper of the car, right next to the worn-looking Ohio license plate. "Good thing they were wearing their swimsuits under their jeans today." She sent Nell a humorous look. "I hope they remembered to leave them on when they were tearing off their clothes before jumping in. At one place we stayed earlier this summer, they didn't." Her lips twitched. "Needless to say, we were quickly asked to move along."

Nell chuckled. Aside from being noisy, she thought the boys seemed pretty well-behaved.

"You should put on a suit and head over there with us," Gardner encouraged. "I bought hot dogs. Thought I'd toss them on that grill that's next to the pool. The boys'll be starving despite the food they get at their summer camp."

Nell's stomach rumbled right on cue. "I don't have a swimsuit."

Gardner looked vaguely scandalized. "That doesn't matter," she said quickly. "I saw Mrs. Goldberg—over there from number eleven?" She pointed with her soda can toward the other wing of the motel. "She was in the pool last week wearing a pair of bright green leggings and a matching long-sleeved T-shirt." She grinned. "She looked like an amphibian with white hair, but what the heck."

Nell laughed. It was hard to resist Gardner's contagious smile. "Maybe."

An outraged yell sounded from the pool area, followed by a squeal and a whole lot of splashing. Gardner stood. "Sounds like refereeing is required." She adjusted her towel over her shoulder and jogged off, her sandals flapping noisily. A few moments later, her raised voice joined those of her sons. "George, how many times have I told you not to pick on Vince?"

Nell let the noise wash over her.

She was thirty-six now. She had no prospects for a relationship, much less one with daddy potential.

But if she didn't start thinking about these things now, when would she?

When it was too late altogether?

Nell and Ros had both gotten birth control implants in their arms several years ago. But even Ros—who was more committed to her career than anyone—was evidently thinking about having a baby. Was she hearing the tick-tock of a biological clock that before neither she nor Nell had believed actually existed?

Was Nell hearing her own clock?

The yelling over at the pool increased in volume and intensity. Nell heard Gardner shout, "Out. Right this minute. All of you!"

Two minutes later, the sopping-wet lot of them

were trooping back across the parking lot. Gardner's beach towel was soaking, too. "Rain check on the hot dogs," she said before she ordered her boys to march their rear ends into the room. The door slammed shut after them, not entirely cutting off their noisy arguments.

Nell looked out over the lights of Weaver again.

Maybe her clock wasn't ticking as loudly as she feared.

The lights lining Main Street had almost all come on now. She followed the glimmering line from New Weaver to old. Then she continued down the line as it dimmed again and disappeared with only an occasional headlight to mark the road's whereabouts. Farther still was where Vivian's mansion was located. And beyond that, the shadowy peaks of Rambling Mountain, where a man named Otis Lambert had lived in a ramshackle cabin on a barely functioning ranch for a considerably long life.

Nell had never met Otis. Everything she knew about the apparently miserly old man she'd learned after his death.

Regardless of what had happened with her career, she was glad that the old man's will had surfaced. Glad that his wishes to donate most of his mountain—either to the state of Wyoming if they'd have it or the town of Weaver if not— would have a chance to be honored. The part of the mountain not being donated, the cattle ranch called the Rambling Rad, had been sold to a Colorado developer—Gage Stanton, with whom Archer had worked for years now. The money from the sale of the Rambling Rad went to the man who'd run the ranch and cared for Otis in his last few years of life. Jed Dalloway had continued taking care of the Rad after Otis died and while the probate had been in Martin's hands, she'd had a few occasions to meet the man. She'd been impressed with his integrity.

Unlike the "long-lost" relative of Otis's who'd surfaced after his death.

If it had been left to Martin's manipulations, the smarmy Louis Snead would have inherited the entire mountain including the ranch, and he would have sold it all off by now to a mining company for his own quick, huge profit.

Even though that hadn't come to pass, Nell still felt guilty by association. She finished her juice and squeezed the thin plastic bottle between her fingers. It crinkled loudly, which helped drown out the sound of the boys still arguing from inside the room next door.

The light fixture above her door gave a few fizzy snaps, then blinked to life.

What she needed to do was worry less about what Martin had been up to and worry more about formulating a plan to get Vivian's library completed.

She took the empty juice bottle inside the room and tossed it in the trash, then pulled her yellow legal pad out of the briefcase that had been sitting in the room untouched since she'd unpacked it three nights ago.

She carried it back to the chair outside because the yelling still going on next door was less noticeable there, and clicked her pen as she studied the Stay/Go list that she still hadn't torn off and thrown away.

She tapped the end of her pen against the pad. On the Go side, she wrote in Vivian's name.

The list was purely pointless, of course.

Nell had already made the move from Cheyenne. Aside from the boxes left in a second-floor storage unit, there was nothing there for her anymore.

She hoped the day that she felt convinced she'd done the right thing would come sooner rather than later.

Sighing a little, she flipped to a clean page and wrote down all of the arguments she could think of supporting the new library. There were very few reasons not to support it. Most had to do with local taxes and finding either an existing building that was suitable or a parcel of land on which to build one.

To Nell's mind, raising the necessary funds seemed the least of the hurdles. For one, Vivian had already raised nearly half of the estimated cost. If she hadn't realized the importance of a buy-in from the entire community, she would have already personally donated the rest of the needed capital.

When she became really frustrated with the project's progress, Nell knew it took considerable self-control on Vivian's part not to simply throw more money on the table with the expectation that it would flatten any hurdles standing in her way.

And while that was often true in some places, it wasn't necessarily true right here in this small town.

She heard her cell phone ring and only then noticed that the argument next door had finally ceased. She pushed out of her seat again and went inside to grab her phone. She glanced at the name on the display before she answered. "Good evening, Vivian," she greeted.

Her new boss didn't mince words. "Do you have a cocktail dress? Or just a closetful of those shapeless suits you're always wearing?"

Nell winced. She couldn't help sliding a look toward the bar where she'd hung three of her work suits. She turned her back on them and returned to her salmon-colored chair. "Why do I need a cocktail dress?"

"I've decided to have a little soiree on Friday evening for the town council members. It'll be here at the house, of course."

Nell grimaced. Bugs had begun buzzing around the light above her head. She swiped at a moth that flew past her face. "Are you certain that's wise, Vivian?" Nell was certain it was not, but she also wasn't sure her boss of two days was ready for such bluntness to begin going both ways.

"Why wouldn't it be wise?"

The moth flew past Nell's face again and she waved her hand at it, grimacing when her wrist made contact with the chalky body.

She gave up the fight against nature and went inside the room again. She didn't close the door, but she did turn off the lamp so as not to draw the beasties inside. "Because of the optics," she told Vivian as she wet a washcloth and wiped off her wrist. "Even though the library seems like an effort that the entire community would support, the council members need to be objective. Or at least give the appearance of remaining objective. If they don't, they'll be out of their positions when the next vote occurs in September."

"I ran a few years ago," Vivian said. "I nearly won, too."

Nell was glad Vivian couldn't see her smile over the obvious consternation in her boss's tone. "You didn't want to try again?"

"I decided there were better ways to accomplish what I want than by sitting on a dreary committee. But had I won, I would have kept Squire Clay from doing so. He still holds the seat he won against me. You can relax, though, because I'm not intending to bribe any of the council members."

Nell was glad Vivian couldn't see her wince.

"And you still haven't answered my question. Cocktail dress. Yes or no?"

"No," she admitted. "I don't have a cocktail dress."

"Get one. There's no time to call one of my designers but you can visit Classic Charms."

Designers? Nell shook her head a little as the thought lodged in her brain.

"It's on Main Street not far from the sheriff's office," Vivian continued. "An odd little shop, but I've found what it carries at the very least to be of good quality. Montrose can give you the exact address."

Montrose, whose attitude darkened toward Nell with every task that Vivian put on his plate. As if Nell were the one at fault.

"I know where it's located." She was still a little distracted by the fact that Vivian had *designers*. "I drove by it twice today." There had been an eclectic collection of furniture in the storefront window. Learning they had clothes was something of a surprise.

"Tell them to establish an account with your name on it and send the bill to me. Come in tomorrow after you've taken care of that. I won't need you in the morning for anything else."

Before Nell had a chance to respond, Vivian ended the call.

Nell looked at her screen, not entirely sure she hadn't simply lost the connection.

When the phone vibrated again a moment later, she decided she'd been right. "Sorry I lost you."

"You've never lost me, Cornelia," a deep voice said.

Nell's phone slid from her suddenly nerveless fingers, landing on the bed. She eyed the screen that bore a number that was *not* Vivian Templeton's, but instead belonged to the woman's grandson.

"I thought you were Vivian," she told Archer when she'd picked up the phone again. She flipped on the lamp because talking to Archer while sitting in the dark just didn't seem like a thing she ought to do. "What do you want?"

"Still haven't learned the art of pleasant chit-chat, have you?"

A moth dared to enter the room and she swatted the air around it with her legal pad, encouraging it to reconsider. "Archer," she said warningly.

"How's it going with the cat?"

The moth flew up to the ceiling and landed there, upside down.

She really hated moths.

"The food is getting eaten by something," she allowed. "But I'm still not convinced it's being eaten by your mysterious cat." She kicked off her tennis shoes and climbed up onto the mattress. It was overly soft and dipped deeply wherever she placed her feet, which meant it was an exercise in balance just to keep from tipping over.

"Tired of driving out there yet?"

She steadied herself with her fingertips against the wall above the fake-wood slab of a headboard and stretched higher with the pad of paper. But the moth was still out of reach. "I'm not tired of anything except your harping about it." She went up on her toes to try again but missed when the moth flitted a couple of inches farther away.

Nell's precarious stance wobbled. Her shoulder hit the wall and her breath rushed out of her lungs.

She was pretty sure the moth was taunting her.

"What the hell are you doing?"

"Nothing." When the phone refused to stay tucked between her shoulder and ear, she hit the speaker button and tossed the phone down onto the bed. "I have a moth in my room."

"At Vivian's?"

"Just because you talked about all the rooms

she has doesn't mean I'm automatically using one of them." She gingerly adjusted her stance on the mattress and tossed her notepad toward the moth. She didn't really want to smash it and leave moth bits clinging to the ceiling. That was as unappealing as having a living one clinging to the ceiling. She just wanted it to decide to go elsewhere.

The pages fluttered and the notepad plummeted downward, knocking into the lampshade and sending it askew. The moth's wings didn't move an inch. The chalky thing remained right where it was.

"You found an apartment already? That was fast."

She gave the moth a baleful look.

The jouncing of the mattress had sent her phone skittering off the side and onto the outdated shag carpet. She hopped off the bed. "I'm at the Cozy Night," she said a little breathlessly. She moved the phone to the nightstand, ignoring the blue oath her announcement earned.

"Does my grandmother know that?"

Nell wrinkled her nose at the phone as if he were able to see her. "I haven't hidden it if that's what you're implying."

He swore again, sounding genuinely irritated. "I'm not implying anything. The Cozy Night's a dive."

Annoyance bubbled inside her, too. "Just because it's not up to *your* lofty standards doesn't mean there is a single thing wrong with it. It's clean, affordable and—"

"—and riddled with moths."

She glared up at the grayish body clinging to the ceiling. "*One* moth," she argued, "and they throw themselves against lights in even the finest places." She yanked her hair out of her eyes, feeling like she wanted to yank it out of her skull. "And how is it that I get drawn into *the* most ridiculous debates with you?"

"Because you're lucky?"

"Is there anything else you wanted, Archer? Besides my assurance that I'm feeding your invisible cat, that is."

"If you only—" He broke off with a sound that she didn't have a hope of interpreting. "No," he finally said. "There's nothing else."

She picked up the phone, moistened her lips. "Then good night, Archer." Before she could second-guess herself, she brushed her finger over the screen, ending the call.

And told herself she imagined hearing "for now" in the moment before the phone disconnected.

Chapter Six

"Everything good in Weaver?"

They were sitting in Gage Stanton's Denver office and Archer looked over at his friend. He was sitting behind his desk, feet propped on the edge as he continued making notes on the Rambling Mountain material that he and Archer had been reviewing all that day.

"No." He pocketed his phone and plucked a slice of pizza from the box that Gage's secretary had delivered earlier before she'd left for the day. "But it's good enough."

He didn't like the idea of Nell staying at that

cheap motel but he didn't know how on earth he'd be able to change the situation.

Irritated with himself as much as with her, he sank his teeth into the pizza and tore off the tip. The slice was cold. Colder now than the bottle of beer he'd been nursing for the last hour.

Gage dropped his feet to the floor. He scrubbed his hand down his face and tossed aside his pen. "Why did I think it was a good idea to develop a guest ranch on Rambling Mountain?"

"Because you're a sucker for a pretty face?"

Gage grunted. "Sucker for a good employee who has defected on me, more like." He reached for his own slice of cold pizza. "April quit working for me more than a month ago, remember? She's busy with Jed now planning their wedding. She dumped all that money into this guest ranch business and can't think about anything else except orange blossoms and wedding dresses."

Archer figured that was somewhat of an exaggeration.

He knew the wedding planning was well in the works, all right. He'd gotten the invitation from April Reed a few weeks ago with her handwritten note saying that she fully expected him to be there to help her and Jed celebrate.

Or else.

Typical April. If it weren't for her, Gage would have scrapped his interest in the mountain that

Otis Lambert had owned and moved on by now. And Archer, who'd been on retainer with Stanton Development for years now, would be focusing on something else that wasn't a constant reminder of Nell Brewster.

When the ailing Otis Lambert had contacted Gage earlier that year, the developer had immediately started envisioning one of his trademark luxury resorts on Rambling Mountain—which had always been privately owned land. But once Otis died, ostensibly intestate, Gage had determined that the development wasn't worth the cost—not after he'd learned there was a mining company prepared to outbid him.

But April—who'd been sent to Weaver by Gage in hopes of getting a jump on the deal—had instead fallen hard for Otis's right-hand man, Jed Dalloway.

Then Otis died and it looked as though a distant relative of his would inherit it all. Gage had determined then that the development wasn't worth the cost—not after he'd learned about the mining company's interest.

April, though, had other ideas. Jed had worked Lambert's mountain ranch, and once his boss's will had actually been found, it was clear that Lambert had wanted the proceeds from the sale of the Rambling Rad to go to Jed. Otis also—despite a lifetime of hoarding the rest of his mountain—had bequeathed everything except the ranch to the state of Wyoming for the purpose of establishing a state park.

Rather than see the man she'd fallen for lose the home that had come to mean so much to him, April convinced Gage to reconsider his interest in the mountain ranch. Instead of razing it all and starting fresh—which had been his initial idea—she talked her boss into saving it. She'd even kicked in her own trust fund to sweeten the deal and ensure that he succeeded.

Now, instead of a luxury resort, Gage was looking down the barrel of a guest ranch plan for a property that clung to the side of the Wyoming mountain. And a guest ranch was something he'd be the first to admit he knew nothing about. Jed and April were set to live on the ranch, with Jed running the operations the same way he had when Otis was alive, but adding in the element of guests.

It was the type of nightmare that hazard insurance agents salivated over.

The ranch sale still hadn't made it through all the red tape, and the state's powers that be still hadn't decided whether they could—or even wanted to—establish a new state park with the rest of the land. If that answer turned out to be a polite "no thank you," then the responsibility for the mountain would be tossed squarely into the lap of the town of Weaver.

Either way, Otis's intention was that his pristine land become available for public use. And people *would* come to Rambling Mountain. It was a sportsman's paradise just waiting to happen. Whether they stayed at the planned guest ranch to play at herding cattle and God only knew what, or crowded into dive motels like the Cozy Night in Weaver, they would come.

It was simply a matter of time.

But until then, Gage was keeping Archer busy navigating through all the moving parts, hedging against the worst-case scenarios while laying groundwork for the best-case one.

Generally, Archer appreciated a challenge. But his mind kept drifting away from the business at hand to Nell.

He didn't exactly blame her for it, but he wasn't thrilled by the distraction.

Until Lambert's will was discovered, she'd been assisting the attorney assigned to administer the estate. She'd also unexpectedly been the one to give Archer the heads-up that Winemeier Mining was working with Louis Snead, who would have inherited the land if not for that will being found, literally at the eleventh hour. Snead, whose only interest in his dearly departed relative was the mountain, would have signed off on a sale to the mining company while the ink was still drying on the court's decision. If that had happened, the mountain would have been sliced and diced until none of its natural resources remained.

Archer still was surprised by Nell's actions. Not that she'd been breaking any rules. There'd been no confidentiality breach. But all the same, she'd approached him. And usually, she avoided him even more than his stepsister did. She had ever since he'd made the mistake of making more out of their furtive friendship than she had.

"I need something stronger than a warm beer," he muttered, more to himself than the other man.

"Amen to that." Gage immediately shoved away from his desk and stretched as he stood. "The lounge or my place?"

"The lounge," Archer said immediately. It was three floors down from Gage's high-rise office. Closer than his penthouse that was five floors up.

It helped that the man owned Stanton Tower from the ground floor to the top.

They took the elevator down to the restaurant, which in reality was one of the best in the city. And—not surprisingly—also owned by Gage Stanton.

Gage greeted the hostess as they passed her on the way to the private club where one needed an official invitation to enter. There were a few patrons sprinkled around the tables. Nobody gave them any attention as they walked through to the open-air patio hugging the corner of the building.

They'd barely sat down when an attractive woman in a svelte black dress appeared. She set a tray on the low table between them. "Shall I bring your usual, Mr. Stanton?" She directed the question to Gage, but her eyes slid over Archer.

"As soon as possible, Theresa. Thanks."

Theresa immediately glided away and Gage reached for one of the fancy little appetizers on the tray she'd left. He popped it in his mouth and pulled out a pack of cigarettes. He extracted one and rolled it between his fingers as if he were savoring the feel of it.

Archer had yet to see his old friend actually light up one of the cigarettes he always carried. "You're not that worried about the guest ranch, are you? We can bring in an expert to consult. I've already been looking into some of the more successful outfits out there. There's a place called Angel River near the Wyoming-Montana border that's been winning awards for years with rates just as high or higher than some of your resorts. Pretty swell setup. Definitely not all sleeping on straw beds and shoveling manure. And if you can talk Jed and April into adding a smaller winter resort at the summit as well—" He spread his hands, wordlessly.

"I know I'm not going to lose money with you

watching out for things," Gage said a little drily. Then he rubbed his forehead like there was a pain there. "Noah's in rehab again."

Understanding hit. Noah was Gage's younger brother and he'd been in and out of treatment for years. "Thought he'd been doing pretty well."

"So did I." Gage held up the cigarette and eyed it expressionlessly for a moment before slipping it back inside the pack that he pocketed once more. He rubbed his forehead again. "I don't know what to do about him," he admitted.

"Maybe don't do anything," Archer suggested bluntly. "He's a grown man."

"He's a spoiled kid in a grown man's body," Gage corrected wearily. "All he has ever cared about is himself." He fell silent while Theresa delivered their drinks. When she disappeared again, he looked at Archer. "Thought you and Theresa weren't seeing each other anymore."

"We aren't." He sipped the scotch and it hit the back of his throat with welcome warmth.

"She's sure giving you the looks."

"Is she?" Archer hadn't really noticed. He sank deeper into the thick cushions of his chair. Gage never did anything halfway. Everything he surrounded himself with was first-rate.

He was also one of the hardest-working fools Archer had ever known.

Gage had been raised by a single mom who'd

worked for a pharmaceutical magnate. If he'd ever known his father, he'd never said. He'd earned every bit of success he had, whereas his little half brother, Noah, had never had to work for a single thing thanks to being the only child of that pharmaceutical magnate.

Money. It could bring out the best in people. So often, though, it brought out the worst.

Archer looked up at the inky sky. Thought about Nell. About the night he'd brought her home from The Wet Bar.

The only reason he'd put her in the guest room bed was because she'd been drunk enough to climb into *his* bed, first.

It would have been way too easy to take advantage of that situation.

If he were honest with himself, he very nearly had.

Only the ringing of his phone had brought him to his senses. He'd dragged Nell's arms from around his neck. Somehow managed to button her back into her clothes and literally dumped her into the guest room. The only reason she'd stayed there was because she'd finally, mercifully passed out.

When—*if*—he was going to go down that rabbit hole with Nell again, he wanted her fully aware that she'd chosen to go down it with him, too.

"My grandmother's having a party on Friday," he told Gage abruptly. Before Archer had phoned

Nell, Vivian had called him specifically to let him know she expected him to be there regardless of how much rearranging of his schedule it might entail.

It wasn't the first time it had dawned on him that he was surrounded by a lot of strong-willed women with expectations where he was concerned.

"It's for that library project of hers," he went on, "but if the mountain ends up under Weaver control—and my hunch is that it's leaning that way—it'd be an opportunity for you to start making some connections with the locals."

Gage was shaking his head. "That's what I've got you for."

It wasn't the first time Gage had avoided going to Weaver. Archer knew it couldn't be because of Gage's ex-wife, Jane, who lived there. Gage had staked Jane in her purchase of a local bar and grill and admitted more than once that they were far happier with each other's company as exes than they'd ever been during the few years they'd been married more than a decade earlier.

"I already know the power players in Weaver," Archer countered. "That's not the point. They're going to want to know *you*. Know who they'll be inviting into their world. Once all the dust is settled about the mountain, what you do on it is going to change things for that town, and they all know it. Tourism is a whole new ball of wax for that area."

"Then I'll do the meetings I need to do." Gage's lips twisted a little. "But what I don't need to do is crash your grandmother's party. I've already donated money to her library deal."

"Afraid she'll ask you for more?"

Gage's expression finally lightened. "Now you've got it."

Theresa returned and leaned close to Gage, murmuring in his ear. He didn't react, but when she was gone again, he slammed back the rest of his drink and stood. "Ever think about finding an island where the only things to worry about are which hammock makes for the most comfortable nap?"

Archer shook his head. "Nope." Still, he was the man's attorney. If there was a problem that needed his expertise, it was his responsibility to handle it. "Anything I can help with?"

"Just business," Gage dismissed. "Stay and enjoy yourself," he said before he strode away.

"I plan to," Archer murmured. He popped three of the little fancy crackers into his mouth and pulled out his phone. It wasn't often he voluntarily called his stepsister. She was definitely a strong-willed woman, but when it came to Archer, Rosalind's only expectation was that he stay out of her way.

But he had enough scotch warming his belly to blunt the edge.

Amazingly, she answered on the fourth ring. "Archer." Her voice was cool. "I'm in the middle of something, so this better be important."

"What's going on between you and Nell?"

He could hear the very loud irritation in her silence. "I have nothing to say to you about that," she finally said, in what he considered an alarmingly polite way. She usually told him to do the physically impossible before she'd hang up on him.

Which meant there *was* something more going on than a simple parting of the ways. "She's living in a third-rate motel in Weaver, Ros. You saying you don't care about that?"

"I don't care about that," she echoed flatly. "So you can go f—"

"Now, now, now," he cut her off. "Don't say anything you might really mean." He poked through the delicacies displayed on the tray. "You know every time we speak, I have to remind myself that you carry Meredith's genes in you, because the older we get, the only ones you show are the ones you got from your dad."

"What do you want me to say, Archer?" She actually sounded pained. "There's nothing I can do to help her. Nell chose her side."

"And I'm asking you why! Why are there sides

when you've been friends for better than twenty years? I know Martin's at the root of whatever it is." Ros, ironically enough, was a stickler for fairness. At least where people beyond her own family were concerned. She wouldn't stoop to spreading rumors and innuendo about an enemy, much less Nell. Whereas those tactics were exactly what Martin would do, even to his own family.

The fact that Meredith hadn't been able to keep custody of Ros when she'd managed to escape him was proof of that.

His stepsister's silence turned stony. It was all too easy to picture the face that went along with it.

He exhaled wearily. "I'm not your enemy, kiddo. No more so now than when we were young." When he was being raised with his sisters by her mom and his dad—a boisterous, secure and happy family—and she was stuck alone with Martin. Even then, he'd known she was envious, just as he'd known she'd blamed Meredith for that situation more than she'd ever blamed her father. Such was the effectiveness of Martin Pastore's manipulations. "You can talk to me if you've got a probl—"

"Goodbye, Archer," she cut him off, and hung up on him.

Theresa chose that moment to sit down on the arm of his chair and trail her fingertip along his forearm. "You're looking a little lonely sitting out here, Archer."

He slowly looked up from the swirling screen-saver that had appeared on his phone to her face. "Then I'd better do something about that." He finished off his drink and gave her a pat on the arm as if he were her uncle before standing and making his own exit.

He kept his own apartment in the city not far from Gage's building. After he'd retrieved his files from Gage's office, he stopped at his place and grabbed a few more files that he added to the box he kept in his truck. He left a message for Jennifer, who ran his office with far more skill than he'd ever shown, and was on the highway thirty minutes after leaving Theresa.

It was well after midnight when he reached Braden. He considered driving through to Weaver and the Cozy Night. But if he went to Nell now and forcibly removed her from that particular hole-in-the-wall, she'd think he was just as crazy as he felt.

It was the only reason why he turned off the highway when he reached the narrow road that led to his house. He drove between the stone pillars of the gate he never closed and soon after, he was home, walking through the darkened rooms until he reached his bedroom.

He tossed himself down on the bed still fully

dressed and closed his eyes, happy to fall into familiar dreams where Nell never pushed him away.

The cat food bowl was empty again.

Nell propped her hands on her hips and looked around, but all she saw were the same things that she'd seen the day before. Only this time, she was seeing it through the beams of her car headlights.

Vivian had kept her busy that afternoon. And that evening.

Which meant that the scrubby brush now looked more gray than green. The boulders were nothing more than black shadows and the wildflowers were only an occasional flash of yellow if the breeze sent them swaying at the right angle to catch her headlights.

All cats were nocturnal, weren't they?

"Here kitty, kitty, kitty," she called softly, feeling a little foolish. Any stray who was out here coming around to eat food off the top of a stone pillar was probably not the kind of feline that'd come at a call.

She peered beyond the beams of light, but saw nothing more than before.

She tipped the cat food bag from her back seat over the bowl. It wasn't a very large bag and she would need to buy more soon because it was going to be empty in a couple of days. With the bowl full again, she stood on her toes to return it to its usual spot.

When she went back down on her heels, she glanced around again, then went stock-still at a tall shape in the distance out of range of the head-lights.

No cat stood that tall.

Her heart shot up into her throat and she felt en-tirely incapable of movement while every monster movie she'd ever seen whizzed through her mind.

She was the worst sort of monster movie vic-tim. The kind whom she and Ros had always yelled at at the movies for showing their stupid-ity so clearly. For not turning and at least *trying* to escape.

The shape grew larger and she felt sweat crawl down her spine. The thick paper of the cat food bag crinkled loudly when her fingers tightened on it. The bag wasn't much of a weapon, but if she threw it at the beast—it obviously couldn't be a monster movie one, but who knew what sort of an-imals besides stray kitties came out after dark?—maybe it would be warning enough to send it off in another direction.

She bounced on the toes of her low-heeled pumps, hearing her heart pound inside her head, and when the shape gained yet a little more sub-stance, she balled up the bag as tightly as she could and launched it wildly in the air. Then she raced back to her car, practically diving head-first inside it.

She yanked the door closed and shoved the car into Reverse, backing away from the pillars in preparation of turning around. Whatever was out there—mountain lion or worse—was welcome to the kibble.

Nell would buy another bag and make sure she didn't come out here again except when it was still light.

She shifted out of Reverse and started to turn the car, but the shape was barreling toward her and when it crossed her headlights, she realized that it wasn't an animal at all.

It was Archer.

She shoved the car into Park and launched out of the car, barreling right back toward him. She reached the pillars at the same time that he did, and shoved her hands against the solid plane of his chest.

The fact that he was laughing infuriated her even more.

"You're supposed to be in Denver! You scared the peanuts out of me!" She went to shove him again, but he was leaning over, hands on his thighs as he laughed even harder.

"I thought you were a bear or something!" She kicked at the ground, which was covered with the kibble that had sprayed out of the bag when she'd thrown it.

He closed his hand over her shoulder, holding her in place. His face was pale in the headlights but the broad smile on his face was brilliant. "And you what? Thought you'd ward off the bear with kitty kibble?"

She kicked more nuggets of said kitty kibble over his legs. Now that her silly panic was assuaged, she didn't want to acknowledge the smile struggling to get free. "I thought you were out of town," she repeated.

"I was." He was still cupping her shoulder and when he turned and gestured with his other hand into the darkness beyond the headlights, his arm just seemed to naturally slide around her shoulders altogether. "My truck's parked right over there. How'd you miss it?"

She shrugged his arm off before too many of her cells could remember how much they liked the contact. "Maybe because I was concentrating on feeding a cat that I don't even believe exists!" She let out a loud breath and tugged at the hem of her blouse that had escaped her waistband. "But now you're back, which means I am off that particular hook." She started marching back to her car.

"Oh, come on, Nell." Archer followed her. "Relax. Come on up to the house at least. I was just about to put a steak on the grill when I saw your headlights." He caught her hand as she reached for the door.

"It's late and I have things to do." She ignored the warmth streaking up her arm.

"What things? Fighting moths?"

She let out a frustrated sound. "It doesn't matter what things!"

"Then whatever they are can wait." He squeezed her hand slightly. Cajoling. "Come on. You can fill me in on Vivian's project. I worry about her."

The sound she let out then was nothing but pure scoff. "Vivian's the last person you need to worry about. She runs circles around everyone."

"Yeah." His thumb brushed a small, distracting circle over the back of her hand. "But she also has an inoperable brain tumor, so humor me."

It took a moment for the words to penetrate. "I... *What?*"

"She wouldn't appreciate me telling you, either. She prefers to choose who, and when, she shares that information with so try not to throw me under the bus next time you see her."

No longer in the line of the headlights, all she had to see him by was the light from inside her car and the proliferation of stars punctuating the sky overhead. She peered hard at him. "You're not joking."

"Not about that."

She let out a long, long breath. "A tumor."

"Yes, a tumor. Fortunately, it's small and hasn't caused any bad episodes in over a year, but there are no guarantees. It's a situation that could turn on a dime. Anytime. Anywhere. She has tests every few months, monitoring it."

Nell finally tugged her hand away from him and ducked into the car. She turned off the engine and it ticked softly in the sudden silence.

Her mother had died of a brain aneurysm.

No warning. No preparation.

She closed her eyes for a moment. The car engine ticked twice more.

Then she straightened again, closed the door and faced him. "I hope you have two steaks, because I haven't had a chance to eat all day."

Chapter Seven

"Could have pulled your car up to the house," Archer told her for the third time when they reached the house after a fair piece of walking. "It would have saved you walking all that way in those plain Jane grandma shoes of yours."

She huffed. She'd chosen the shoes because they were leather with chunky heels of a sensible height that worked perfectly for an associate lawyer who usually was racing from one courtroom to another. She'd owned them for years and had already had them resoled. Twice. "If I were wearing shoes like *your* grandmother wears, I would have." So far, Nell hadn't seen Vivian wear the same shoes twice. They were all quite high-heeled, and they all screamed "designer."

"Yeah, she does like her shoes, doesn't she?" He took two steps in one as he vaulted up the wood stairs near the corner of the house.

She'd seen the structure only from a distance up to now, of course. She still hadn't seen a guest-house at all, which made her think he'd made that up just to yank her chain.

It would be typical Archer behavior.

She followed him up the steps to the wood deck lining the front three sides of the house, past a fancy gas grill that put the little charcoal thing next to the pool at the Cozy Night to shame, and through a door that opened into his kitchen.

It was hard not to gape a little, because it looked like a kitchen that actually got used. A lot.

Not because it was messy, though there were a few dishes stacked in the sink, but because the pots hanging from a rack over the stove looked slightly worn. Well used. Because there was a jug of utensils—mismatched ones—sitting next to the gas stove. The ones tucked inside a fancy stone container that had sat next to the stove in the condo she'd shared with Ros had all been carefully matched and had stayed that way for the simple reason they'd never been used.

A rustic loaf of bread sat on a scarred cutting board and the coffeepot—the real kind, not one of the fancy pod deals that she was used to—sat on a cast-iron stove grate.

There was a farmhouse sink, a doublewide stainless steel refrigerator and a sturdy wood table in the middle of the room. The counters were butcher block, the floors were slate, and the colorful modern painting hanging on one wall was probably an original.

She peered at the slanted signature in one corner below the swirl of squiggles covering the canvas. Soliere.

She'd never heard of the artist. But that didn't mean anything. She'd never bothered with art studies. She'd been more interested in passing the bar exam.

Feeling bemused, she set her car keys on the table. "This is, ah—"

He waited, eyebrows raised, and she felt her cheeks flush. "Is…what?"

"Nice," she finished a little helplessly.

His lips twitched. "Meredith would thank you."

Meredith. His stepmother. Ros's mother.

For some reason, it relieved Nell to know he'd had help with the kitchen. As if he, too, might share some of her kitchen incompetence.

"How *is* Meredith?" She'd first met Ros's mother when she'd been a teenager. But the last time she'd seen her had been at least a few years ago.

"Happily wallowing in grandparenthood." His

tone was dry. "Every one of my sisters is diligently practicing the 'be fruitful and multiply' thing these days. Well, except for Rosalind."

"Wouldn't be too sure about that," Nell murmured.

He gave her a quick look. "Ros is pregnant?"

"No." Then she shook herself. "Not that I know of, anyway." It hurt to think that as things stood now with Archer's sister, Nell would be the last one with whom Ros would share that sort of news. "She mentioned that her boyfriend was interested in starting a family. That's all."

Archer looked thoughtful for a moment. Then his eyes glinted as he rested his hand on the refrigerator door. "Interest you in something to drink?" He waited a beat. "Champagne?"

She gave him a look. She needed no reminder that her last interlude with champagne had landed her in his guest room. "Water is fine," she over-enunciated. And had a flash of Montrose's face in her mind as a result.

Archer's smile twitched and he reached into a cupboard instead of the fridge. He filled the glass he pulled out with water from the tap and set it on the table next to her car keys. "There is something else I need to break to you, though." His voice turned serious.

Unease crept through her. Something worse

than his grandmother's brain tumor? "What?" Caution practically dripped from her voice.

"I only have the one steak."

Her shoulders sagged as unease trickled away. "You are—" she jabbed her finger into his shoulder "—impossible."

"It's a big one, though," he said as if she hadn't spoken at all. "One of those cowboy cuts."

She didn't know a cowboy cut from a finger cut. But she did know that her stomach was growling.

She rubbed her palms down the sides of her skirt. It had already been so late when she'd gotten away from Vivian's that she hadn't wanted to take the time to change before driving out here to feed the cat. "Is there somewhere I can wash up?"

He looked like he wanted to start laughing again. "Worried I don't have indoor plumbing?"

"If you don't stop laughing at me, you can start worrying what I might do to you if I get my hands on one of those pots hanging behind you."

"I don't laugh at you, Cornelia. I laugh with you."

She gave him a deadpan stare. "Am I laughing? I wasn't aware."

He chuckled and gestured over his shoulder toward a darkened doorway. "Second door on the left."

She went through the doorway and startled when a softly golden light automatically went on.

A farmhouse with tech.

Trust Archer Templeton to have it.

She found the bathroom and washed up, staring at her reflection in the oval mirror hanging above the pedestal sink. He obviously had a predilection for them. She didn't care how many pedestal sinks he had in however many bathrooms.

She just needed to remember she shouldn't have a predilection for *him*.

She returned to his kitchen, resolutely keeping her curiosity about the rest of his house under control. He was standing at the butcher-block counter wielding a knife, and for a moment she watched the play of muscles beneath his shirt.

She moistened her lips, hovering there, feeling warm inside. Why, *why* did he have to be the one to ring those bells?

"Don't just stand there," he said without looking around at her. "Salad makings are in the fridge. Tomatoes are on the counter in a bowl. In case you don't recognize them, they're the round, shiny red things."

She flushed and yanked open the refrigerator door. Her idea of preparing a salad was to tear open a bag of the premade stuff.

There wasn't any such animal in his fridge, though.

She pulled out a bunch of romaine from the crisper drawer and carried it over to the counter near where he was working. She had seen a cooking show a time or two. Or at least had flipped past a cooking channel on the hunt for something more interesting. She could fake it.

She peeled off the rubber band keeping the lettuce leaves contained and hesitated.

Archer stopped chopping and set a large, holey bowl on the counter next to her. He began chopping again.

Garlic. That she knew simply because of the penetrating aroma. And he already had a neat stack of thinly sliced onions.

She slid her gaze back to her own task at hand and separated one leaf from the rest of its pack. She was as unsuccessful at blocking him out of her peripheral vision as she was blocking out how enticingly companionable it felt to be standing there with him.

She focused even more attention on the lettuce, methodically tearing the leaf into bite-size pieces that she dropped in the bowl. She repeated the process with a couple of more crispy leaves and was feeling quite proud of the precisely sized results. Then she finally ran the bowl under the faucet and shook it as dry as she could get it.

In the same amount of time that she'd taken to tear up a few lettuce leaves, however, Archer had filled his cutting board with a huge mound of chopped vegetables.

His eyes crinkled with amusement when he caught her comparing her small pile with his. "Size doesn't matter."

She managed to keep her response contained to a bored, raised eyebrow. "That's what all men say."

He gave a soundless laugh and swiped half of his cutting board bounty into another bowl. He dropped a pair of salad tongs on top and handed it to her, then carried the cutting board and the rest of its contents, along with the enormous steak, out of the kitchen.

She pressed her tongue against her teeth and eyed the painting on the wall. The squiggly lines racing around the canvas might as well have been the pattern of her crazy heartbeat.

Afraid he'd come back in and find her standing there like that, she hastily dumped her lettuce pieces in with the rest of the veggies and flipped it all around a few times with the tongs.

It was the only kind of salad she really liked. One that was less green stuff and more chunky vegetables. He'd even sliced the kernels off a fresh cob of corn.

The man had probably never poured prepared salad out of a bag in his life.

She set the salad bowl in the center of the table

and then poked around the kitchen enough to find a couple of plates and flatware.

She set them out on the table and then, with no other reason to keep hiding in the kitchen, followed him outside.

He was standing in front of the grill. The sleeves of his shirt were rolled up to his elbows and his shirttails were hanging loose over his jeans.

She had a mad desire to slide her hand beneath the shirttail and run her palm up the length of his spine. To discover if his skin still felt as warm and supple where it stretched over sinewy muscle as she remembered.

She lifted her glass so fast to take a drink that she managed to spill water down her chin and the front of her blouse in the process.

"Having a problem there?"

She wanted to sink through the deck and the Wyoming earth beneath.

She swiped her chin and set the glass on the wide beam of wood at the top of the deck railing. The steak was sizzling on one side of the grill, sending up a delicious aroma that had her mouth watering. At least she hoped it was the primary reason behind that particular reaction.

Yes, Archer was insanely attractive. Always had been. But she flatly refused to believe he could actually make her mouth *water*.

"Want a taste?"

He was holding up a chunk of red bell pepper with grill marks on it and before she could even offer a yay or nay, he'd slid it past her surprised lips.

It was deliciously charred and terribly hot. She chewed quickly, gingerly, chasing it with the rest of the water in her glass. "Give a girl some warning," she managed when she finally swallowed. But then she ruined her protest by stepping closer to him and the grill. "Can I have another one?"

On the other half of the grill, he'd dumped the vegetables atop a thick piece of foil and was slowly turning them with the tines of a long-handled fork. He jabbed another chunk of pepper and handed it to her.

She carefully took it from the fork, holding it between her fingertips. While she waited for the morsel to cool a bit, she studied him from beneath her lashes. "When did Vivian discover she had a tumor?"

"Before she moved to Weaver," he answered immediately. "I think it's what prompted her to come to Wyoming. Feeling her mortality. Wanting to set things right between her and my father and uncle."

Because of the summer after her mom died when she'd accompanied Ros on her forced visitation with Meredith, Nell knew enough about his family to remember that his father, Carter, was a retired insurance agent and his uncle was a pediatrician. And that they'd lived in Wyoming for as long as Ros knew, anyway. "Why did things need to be set right?"

"Vivian wasn't always the philanthropic, kindly old lady you know and love."

Nell let out an abbreviated laugh. Vivian was, indeed, philanthropic. But in just the last week Nell had learned the woman was not at all the "kindly old lady" type. She was sharp, decisive and demanding. She also wasn't above manipulation when a situation called for it, which explained the cocktail party that she'd decided to throw.

"It's too early to love, much less claim to know her very well, but I *do* like her," Nell said. "She's a force, just like you said. Kind of hard not to be impressed by her."

"True enough." He adjusted the heat under the vegetables and leaned against the rail next to her.

She told herself it was just coincidence that his hand happened to land on top of hers where it rested on the smooth wood. Particularly when he moved it away again a moment later to fold his arms across his wide chest.

She quickly averted her eyes from the way his shirt tightened around his biceps.

"My father and uncle, on the other hand, find very little to admire about their mother." He crossed one boot in front of the other in a casual stance. "They railed against their rigid upbringing. Blamed her when their father—Sawyer Templeton—died. They had an older brother who took off when he was still a young man and then he died too, and that was yet another thing to blame her for." He dropped his arms and selected his own steaming-hot piece of squash, blowing on it briefly before sinking his teeth into it.

She swallowed, looking down at the toes of her shoes. A dim portion of her mind acknowledged that they really were sort of unflattering.

The rest of her was humming along with the internal tune of jangling bells.

"Anyway," he continued, "none of us even knew Vivian existed until she showed up here out of the blue one day. She'd buried another husband—"

"Dear Arthur."

He nodded. "Dear Arthur. And she said she wanted to make things right. At first, Hayley was the only one who'd have anything to do with her." He shrugged. "Stands to reason, I suppose, my sister being a psychologist and all."

Nell knew that Ros had always been less antagonistic with Hayley than she was with Archer, but then Hayley didn't go out of her way to antagonize their stepsister the way Archer did.

"Vivian even lived with Hayley for a while,"

Archer continued. "She's a good family therapist, but not even she was good enough to heal the rift between Vivian and my dad and uncle."

"Things got better, though. Right? Vivian talks about you and your sisters and cousins all the time."

"It got better with us grandchildren," he allowed. "My dad and Uncle David tolerate her because the rest of us have said they have to. But I doubt they'll ever be able to really let go of the past. Some things run too deep for healing."

"Seems sad to me. Your dad and uncle are missing out on knowing the person she is now."

"It's just the way it is. What would you do if your father suddenly turned up after all these years? If he offered an apology for the way he bailed on you and wanted everything to be hunkydory again?"

The question hit her hard and she winced a little.

"Sorry."

"No." She turned to face him and the grill, though her thoughts were suddenly in the past. "It's a fair enough comparison." She chewed the inside of her cheek for a moment. "I'd be hardpressed to accept it," she admitted eventually.

"There you go," he said quietly. "I'm not going to bust my dad's or my uncle's chops for feeling the way they do. Their relationship with Vivian is different than mine or my sisters' or my cousins'."

She angled her head, studying him for a moment. "You're pretty nonjudgmental for a lawyer. Maybe you should be a judge."

He chuckled. "No thank you. Too much politics to deal with for my taste."

"Yet you're dating Judge Potts." Her stomach churned a little.

"I date lots of women besides Taylor," he countered mildly.

"You're not getting any younger—"

"Flattery. Nice."

"—don't you ever think about getting married?" As nettling as she found her own curiosity, she couldn't seem to stop herself. "Settling down and doing the fruitful-and-multiplying thing yourself?"

"Despite the setups Meredith keeps trying to throw my way, maybe I'm not the settling kind, either."

She felt oddly tense. "You think *I'm* not the settling kind?"

"Are you?" His gaze slid over her face. "How many men have you ever let get under your defenses? And don't say Muelhaupt," he added abruptly. "He's a mouse compared to you."

She made a face. "What is *that* supposed to mean?"

He had the nerve to laugh. "Do you even know how impressively intimidating you are?"

She felt her eyebrows climb up to the middle of her scalp. "Intimidating! If I were the least bit intimidating why am *I* the one who has gotten herself basically banished from Cheyenne for daring to speak the truth?"

Her impetuous words rang out to be quickly absorbed into the night air. But not quickly enough.

And there was nowhere to escape the intensively close look he was giving her. "What truth is that, Cornelia?"

Her mouth ran dry. She opened her lips to say something, but her words failed her.

Telling him what Martin had done would only prove how gullible she'd been. And if she started getting pity from Archer Templeton, she wasn't sure she could stand it.

The sudden flare of fire that streamed into the air from the grill broke the spell and she swallowed, ridiculously relieved when he turned back to the food.

"Get me a couple plates from inside, would you?"

She quickly went inside, grateful for the opportunity to flee even if momentarily. In the seconds it took her to get two more plates and take them out to him, she'd scrabbled together a minimum of composure and he'd conquered the spitting fire.

She held the plates while he transferred the enormous steak to one and the vegetables to the other and then carried them inside while he shut down the grill.

When he found her still standing—hovering—at the table when he came in too, he frowned slightly as he pushed the kitchen door closed.

She almost wished she were somewhere else. "I wasn't sure which spot was yours," she said.

His expression lightened then. "They're all the same, sweetheart." He pulled out the chair closest to him and gestured for her to sit.

She slipped into the seat, but he didn't immediately join her at the table. Instead, he walked out of the room and returned a few moments later with a bottle of wine that he'd already uncorked.

He unceremoniously plunked a clean, stemless glass in front of her and splashed a generous measure of red wine into it. Then he repeated the process for himself and finally took the other chair.

He lifted the glass. "What should we toast to?"

She circled her fingers lightly around her own glass. "Do we have to toast to anything? We could just give it a pass."

"How long has it been since you and I sat down and had a meal together? And I'm not talking about the bar association's annual dinner."

If she really had to, she could calculate it right

down to hours and minutes. "A while," she allowed.

"All right, then." He waited until she lifted her glass also. "To old friends and nonexistent cats."

She gave him an incredulous look. "You cannot really be serious."

His eyes glinted, the green color seeming deeper than ever. "To old friends and unexpected bedfellows."

Her cheeks burned. "To old friends and nonexistent cats," she said crisply.

He smiled and lightly touched the edge of his glass to hers.

When she lifted the glass to her lips, she hoped she was the only one who noticed her hand wasn't entirely steady.

He sliced the enormous steak into two pieces and pushed one of the slabs onto her plate, then followed it up with half of the grilled vegetables despite her protest that she'd never be able to eat that much.

His eyes crinkled. "Sure you can."

And she did.

Afterward, when all of the dishes were empty—except the salad bowl, which was still full—they washed up and Nell gave up trying to stave off that sense of companionability. He poured her a second glass of wine while she dried the few plates they'd used and she sipped at it while he put them away.

And even though she knew she ought to make some move to leave, she kept putting it off.

He showed her around the rest of his house, consisting of three minimally furnished bedrooms—she barely allowed herself to glance into his—an office that was bigger than her room at the Cozy Night and lined with bookshelves crammed with books, a finished basement that housed a gigantic half-moon of a couch and a television that took up nearly an entire wall, the spectacular deck that surrounded three-fourths of the exterior, of course, and yes, even the guesthouse that did exist, after all.

The only reason she hadn't noticed it at first was because it was down a steep hill on the far side of the house, and reached by several steps cut into the hillside.

"Sun rises there," he said, gesturing in that direction. "Best view in the world. And you could still use it. No moths last time I checked."

She looked from the darkened windows of the small guesthouse to his face. "I don't think it's a good idea, Archer."

He made a soft *hmm* sound. "You promised to feed the cat."

"You're here. You feed the cat. You won't even be serious about whether he's real or not."

He dropped his arm over her shoulder. "I'll drive you back to your car."

She tried to refuse but he was adamant. Despite the brilliant moonlight and the bouquet of stars that looked close enough to pluck, it would be too easy to turn an ankle, he said. Too easy to cross paths with a wild animal.

The drive was short. In a matter of minutes, he came to a stop next to her car, right where she'd left it on the other side of the open gate.

She pushed open the truck door and slid out onto the ground. "Didn't see any wild animals," she told him drily, conveniently ignoring her scare when she thought he was one just a few hours earlier.

He draped his wrist over the steering wheel as he looked at her. "I don't want to chance you getting hurt."

Too late.

The words whispered through her mind and had nothing to do with turned ankles or wild animals and everything to do with him.

She stepped away from the truck. "Good night, Archer. Thanks for the steak."

Then she firmly shut the door, climbed quickly into her own car and drove away, grateful that she was the only one who'd ever know the way her heartbeat squiggled around wildly like lines on a canvas.

Chapter Eight

Nell pushed through the door at Ruby's Diner the next afternoon. There was the usual crowd of people waiting for tables alongside the door.

But the occupant of the stool at the counter whom she'd gotten used to seeing was not there at all and she was so surprised that she stopped right in the doorway.

And was promptly bumped into from the rear, and everything she was holding in her arms slid right onto the floor. Pages spilled out of her binder and her purse went sliding.

"Sorry, miss." The bumper crouched down beside her to help as she scrabbled her belongings to-

gether. "Didn't see your brake lights fast enough."
He gathered up a splayed pile of documents, hand-
ing them to her, and she flushed a little.

He was smiling, dark-haired and ridiculously
good-looking.

"It was my fault," she said quickly, taking the
pages and pushing them every which way between
the covers of the binder. She started to straighten
but he beat her to it and took her hand, helping
her up the rest of the way.

She flushed harder, more from knowing they'd
earned the attention of the diners all around them
than because of him. Though he really was attractive. Sort of like an engagingly cute puppy.

"I'm Nick," he said. "Nick Ventura."

His name surprised her even more. "You're
Vivian's architect! The one who's been design-
ing the new library." Her employer hadn't said
just how young her architect was.

His smile widened. "Guilty, I'm afraid. And I
hope one day the library actually makes it off the
page. And you are—"

"Nell Brewster." She adjusted her tenuous
grasp on her belongings again to stick out her
hand. "And I can tell you that she absolutely in-
tends for the library to make it off the page. Vivian hired me to manage the project."

He closed his hand around hers, smiling
warmly. "Then I'll have something more to look

forward to when she calls for design change five hundred and sixty-two."

Nell laughed. "She does have a strong opinion about things that matter to her. I've learned that much." Which was probably the reason why she'd hired an architect before she even had a confirmed location or approval from the town council. "But as it happens, I was going to call you this afternoon. Vivian is having a party this Friday and would like you to do a brief presentation if you're available."

"Have a feeling she'd want me to do it even if I weren't available," he said wryly. "But sure. Whatever she needs."

"Great. Are you here by yourself or—"

He shook his head. "I'm meeting my cousin— ah. Over there." He raised his hand in acknowledgment and Nell automatically glanced over her shoulder to look. A striking woman with graying auburn hair was sipping iced tea while a younger redhead with an animated expression was looking their way.

It was the red hair that caught Nell's attention. She remembered seeing the woman in the courtroom with Archer a few times.

She also remembered the way she'd felt inside witnessing the obviously comfortable way the two related to one another. She'd figured they were involved.

For all she knew, they still were. He'd said it himself. He dated lots of women. Just because Archer was romancing Judge Potts didn't mean he wasn't romancing someone else, too. He'd done it back when Nell had been in law school, after all. She just hadn't known about it at the time.

"Then I should clear the intersection," she told Nick lightly, stepping to one side.

"Why don't you join us? April won't mind—"

"No, no." She shook her head. "Thank you, but I don't want to intrude. And I'm just grabbing a bite. Working lunch, I'm afraid. I'll email you the details about the party." She patted her notebook and began sidestepping toward the counter. "I'm glad we bumped into each other."

"Best collision I've had all year."

She couldn't help but laugh. He was too friendly not to.

She was still smiling when she slipped into the spot between the cash register and Squire Clay's empty seat and dumped her notebook and its disheveled contents on the counter.

Tina immediately greeted her with a wave. "Be with you in a sec, Nell."

"No rush," Nell assured her. She had plenty to keep her busy. She flipped open the binder and began restoring order to it. She'd begun using the notebook to help keep herself organized. She already had sections for fundraising, for construction issues, for permits and approvals. She even had copies of the architectural renderings.

But the section right now at the front of her binder contained her checklists for Vivian's cocktail party being held the following day.

Two items remained unchecked among the dozens of others that were marked off.

A proper dress for Nell.

And a confirmed RSVP from Squire Clay. He was the only holdout from the entire council.

Which was the whole reason she'd come into the diner for lunch in the first place.

She fit the last page onto the binder rings and snapped them closed, then waited until Tina flipped over her coffee cup and filled it before asking about the man's whereabouts. "I thought Squire comes in every day."

"He does." Tina glanced beyond Nell's shoulder and dropped her voice slightly. "But not when she's here."

Nell raised her brows. "When who is here?"

"Gloria." Tina's voice dropped even more. It was nearly soundless. "His wife." She inclined her head an inch. "She's in the corner booth over there with her granddaughter, April."

The corner booth where Nick was now sitting alongside the older woman. A quick sideways glance confirmed it. Nell lifted her coffee cup and took a sip. "He doesn't eat here when his wife eats here?"

"Not since they separated," Tina said under her breath. "It's been the talk of the town all summer."

Nell felt a stab of sympathy for Squire and his estranged wife. She didn't like being the subject of "talk" in Cheyenne. She could only imagine how much worse it would be in such a small town like Weaver.

A peal of laughter erupted from the table in the corner and Nell had to control the urge to look over again. She quickly ordered one of the sandwich specials from Tina before the waitress had to tend her other customers, and flipped to the fundraising section in her binder.

Aside from several corporate donations that had already come in, there was a healthy amount of money that had been contributed by John and Jane Q. Public. But the amount raised still needed to be significantly higher, so in between refereeing the cocktail party appetizer selection battle between Vivian and Montrose, Nell had been looking into possible grant opportunities.

There was one in particular being funded by Swift Oil. And even though the CEO of the company had already made a personal donation—one of the first sizable ones, in fact—Nell didn't see why that should stop her from applying for one of the company's annual philanthropic gifts.

She didn't have a lot of experience with grant writing, but she was willing to try. Swift Oil was headquartered in Braden. The CEO, Lincoln Swift, obviously already recognized that the residents in his town would also benefit by an expanded library in Weaver. She had most of the statistics ready but writing the narrative would take some time. And time wasn't in great supply since the deadline for grant applications to even be considered was tonight at midnight.

She'd printed off the lengthy application on Vivian's printer and had managed to read through it once.

She believed she could get it done in time, but it would be close. And if the library were fortunate enough to win the grant, it would all be for naught if the town council still couldn't agree that it should even be built.

Tina stopped long enough to deliver Nell's sandwich and top off her water glass.

"Where does he—" Nell leaned her head toward the empty seat beside her "—go on days like today when he's avoiding the diner?"

Tina thought about it for a moment. "Honestly, I don't think he goes anywhere. He's probably at home."

"Where's that?"

For a moment, Tina looked surprised. "I keep forgetting that you're not from around here." She glanced toward the corner booth and lowered her voice again. "The Double-C Ranch," she said.

Nell had heard of the ranch, but that didn't mean much. She'd also heard of the Squawking Turkey, too, only to discover the apartment it had offered to rent was little more than a glorified chicken coop. "Can you tell me how to get there?"

"Sure." Tina pulled out a napkin and quickly swiped her pen over it, drawing a few intersecting lines. "Head that way out of town." She jerked her thumb to the left. "Be careful when you take the turnoff. The road is graded but it's still gravel. Once you're off the highway, you'll see the ranch entrance. It's huge. But you'll know you're on the right track."

"Thanks." Nell tucked the impromptu map in her binder and delved inside her purse for her wallet. "Mind wrapping up the sandwich for me, and adding a meat loaf sandwich, as well?"

In answer, Tina whisked away the plate and returned a few minutes later with the two sandwiches neatly packaged. She tucked them inside a paper bag that she handed to Nell. "I don't know why you're so anxious to see him, but good luck."

"Thanks." Leaving enough cash for the bill and tip on the counter for Tina, she gathered everything up and hurried toward the door.

From his spot in the corner, Nick caught her

eye but she didn't linger long enough to do more than return his smile with a quick one of her own.

Following Tina's instructions proved simple enough and before long she was driving though the Double-C entrance, while a cloud of dust billowed behind her in her rearview mirror.

When she finally reached a circular drive that fronted a long, rambling house, the dust clung to every inch of her car. Even though she'd quickly closed her car windows, she felt as if she had dust clinging to every inch of her, too.

With the bag from the diner in hand, she left everything else in the car and approached the massive wooden door at the top of several shallow steps.

She was quickly realizing that the Double-C Ranch wasn't just some regular old cattle ranch.

Not if the outbuildings she could see and the number of vehicles parked around them were any indication. They all bore the same brand that had been burned into the timbers of the ranch entrance.

She used the heavy iron knocker on the door because there didn't seem to be a doorbell. But she eventually had to accept that nobody was coming to answer.

Chewing the inside of her lip, she went back down the steps and started off toward the buildings with all of the vehicles parked outside.

When she reached the first one, she found it to be an office of sorts, with three young women sitting at computers. None of them knew where Mr. Clay might be.

She didn't want to admit defeat. But it was disappointing, even though she'd had no guarantee that he'd be at home.

She left the sandwiches with the girl named Melody, whose desk was closest to the open door of the office. "If you do see him, would you tell him this is from his seatmate Nell at the diner?"

"Sure." Melody didn't seem surprised by the request or anything else where Nell was concerned. She turned her attention back to her computer screen before Nell even turned to leave.

Rather than drive back into town, Nell went to Vivian's place. She parked in the courtyard as usual, but instead of going through the side door there, she circled around to the backside of the house and entered through one of the patio doors where she'd be less likely to run into Montrose.

In that, at least, she was successful. She made it up the stairs in the atrium to the second floor and slipped into the small office she'd taken over not far from where Vivian's was located.

Nell's office didn't look out over Rambling Mountain the way that Vivian's did. In fact, she didn't have any windows at all.

It was still nicer and more spacious than the

cramped quarters she'd occupied at Pastore Legal and there was even an elegant little powder room right next door.

She propped her elbow on the fancy wooden table she was using as a desk and cupped her cheek. She needed to stop thinking about what had been and keep her focus on what was.

A fine idea if she could only manage to follow it consistently.

The phone ringing at her other elbow was a welcome distraction. She answered it with one hand while she pulled a pen from the crystal bowl she'd pressed into service to hold a dozen pens and pencils. She was a little concerned that it might be Lalique or Baccarat crystal, but assumed it wasn't since it had been just sitting around in the conservatory—Vivian actually used that term for her plant-filled sunroom—holding a few cups of potting soil.

"Nell Brewster speaking," she said briskly, then winced a little because that was the way she'd answered the phone at Pastore Legal. And if the caller was a client, she'd immediately begun timing the conversation. Billable hours and all that.

"Thank you for the sandwich."

Squire Clay. Surprise made Nell sit up straighter. "You're welcome." So the sandwich actually had made its way to the man. Melody and her compatriots hadn't seemed overly concerned that it would. "How, uh, how did you know to reach me here?"

"Small town," he said as if that explained it all.

She spun her chair around to stare at the narrow span of wall behind her. There was nothing hanging on it. No artwork. No paintings. She might have repurposed the dirt bowl, but she didn't have enough nerve to commandeer anything else.

She doubted Vivian would care, but Nell wasn't so sure about Montrose. She had no desire to earn his wrath.

Archer's kitchen and his squiggly-lined Soliere drifted through her mind.

She closed off that thought. "I'm sorry I missed you," she told Squire. "But I'm glad the sandwich reached you. I hope it was good."

"Ruby's food always is. Question I've got is why you made that effort at all. Your boss lady's never stooped to sending a pretty filly along to do her dirty work before."

"There's no dirty work," she assured him, trying not to sound stiff. The only dirty work she'd ever been involved in had been because of Martin, unintentional on her part or not, and she didn't appreciate hearing the term now. "I was in the diner this afternoon and missed your company."

He made a soft sort of snort. "You wanted to convince me to show up for the dog and pony *soiree*—" the word dripped with scorn "—that the rest of my council brethren have been suckered into attending."

"I don't think Vivian plans a dog and pony show," Nell countered mildly. "She's only interested in smoothing the way for a new public library. Do you have grandchildren in this community, Squire?"

"Not as smart as you look if you don't already know the answer to that."

He was right. She should have done more homework where he was concerned. As it was, she'd felt a little sideswiped by the impressiveness of his ranch. "A new library only benefits Weaver and the surrounding region. Do you really disagree with that?"

"Only thing I disagree with is the woman you're working for. She doesn't do anything without an ulterior motive."

"I think that could be said of most anyone," Nell pointed out. "In my experience, people's actions almost always have a deeper motive than what is first apparent." She waited a beat, but he didn't reply. Nor did he hang up on her, which she chose to take as encouragement. "I'm no different," she continued. "The first time we met, I could have told you that I'd been hired by Mrs. Templeton. But I knew there was dissension between you when it comes to the library—"

"Not just the library, girl."

She hadn't done her research, so she let that pass, too. "And I was enjoying your company too much to want it ruined. I also realized that if you could get to know me a little before painting me the same color as you've painted her, perhaps you would also have a more open mind when it comes to bringing something really important to this town. You see? Deeper motive."

"Don't have to tell me what's important to this town, either. Been here a hell of a lot longer than she has."

"Yet another reason why it's so important that you exercise your support for it. Do you really think the existing library is adequate?"

He didn't answer that. "Is she going to fire you if you don't get me there tomorrow night?"

Nell winced. She ought to have been prepared for such bluntness. "I certainly hope not. I need the paycheck," she admitted, just as bluntly. Vivian had never mentioned Squire by name. She'd just said she wanted the council there. "But no. I don't feel like it's her intention to hang me out to dry."

"Pays to be cautious where you put your trust, girl."

How well she knew that, too. "And sometimes it pays to go out on a limb despite one's caution," Nell countered. She felt guilt fire in her face, because what limb had *she* ever gone out on? "Particularly when so many others will benefit as a result."

Her little speech was met with silence and she squelched a sigh. "I'm well aware that I'm the new kid on the block, Mr. Clay, and that it's not my place to shower you with platitudes. So let's just leave it that I am glad you enjoyed the sandwich. And I hope one day, I'll share the lunch counter again with you at Ruby's." She didn't wait for a response that she was certain wouldn't be forthcoming anyway, and hung up the phone.

She flipped open her notebook to her checklist and eyed the two incomplete tasks.

She'd struck out on Squire Clay.

That left acquiring a cocktail dress that Vivian Templeton would deem appropriate.

She pinched the bridge of her nose for a moment, then closed her binder again, took it and her purse and cautiously snuck down the staircase so that Montrose with his bat-like hearing didn't notice.

Weaver's current and only library was located in Old Weaver.

That evening, Nell found it easily enough and entered through the swinging glass door. It was the only fairly modern element that the structure possessed. Aside from that, the two-story structure just looked like an old, vaguely Victorian house. Considering she'd been in Weaver nearly a week, she should have done more than just drive by it by now.

Inside, she passed the circulation desk. The teenage boy manning it was engrossed in a thick novel and didn't even look up at her.

That was okay. She wasn't there to check out any materials. She wasn't even there to judge for herself whether the facility was too out of date for the town. The reason she was there was to escape the noise coming from the motel room next to hers while she worked on the Swift Oil grant application.

At the motel, Gardner's car had been gone, meaning that she was working the evening shift at Udder Huddle. Her three boys had been left to stay in the motel room where they'd been in fine form, whooping and hollering over the video game they'd been playing.

The noise had been clear through the walls. They hadn't been misbehaving. They hadn't been fighting. There'd been no reason for her to try to squelch their natural exuberance just because she'd found it difficult to concentrate.

Now that she *was* in the library, though, Nell couldn't stop herself from wandering the aisles, pulling out a book here and there. Paging through it. Lifting the book close to her face and just inhaling the smell of the pages.

She loved that smell.

It always reminded her of her mother.

However, she had a task to complete and wandering among the stacks wasn't going to get it done.

There were only two study desks that she found, and one had bright yellow caution tape strapped all over it because of a broken leg.

Fortunately, the other was not broken and she sank down on one of the hard wooden chairs surrounding it. She flipped open her binder and pulled out the application form, spreading it across the table in front of her. She uncapped her bright yellow highlighter. The instructions were lengthy. Detailed. She wanted to be sure she didn't miss a single thing, because she knew the quickest way to have an application tossed out was for it to have been submitted without every instruction followed.

She read through it once, highlighting the key elements with her marker. When she was done, almost the entire sheet was yellow.

"You always did have a heavy hand with the highlighters."

Nell stared up stupidly at Archer, who'd appeared seemingly out of nowhere to stand beside her table. She frowned at him. "Aren't you supposed to be cat-sitting somewhere?"

His eyes crinkled slightly and he dragged a

chair from the adjacent side of the table and strad-
dled it right there next to Nell. "What're *you* working on?"

She would have liked to produce some reason
not to tell him, but there wasn't one. Not a good
one, anyway. "Swift Oil annually awards a couple
major grants. This year they're both focused on
education. I figure the library fits the bill."

"That explains this." He lifted the edge of the
mostly yellow page. "But it doesn't explain why
you're doing it here." He made a point of swiveling
his head around at the stacks surrounding them.

"Three boys in the motel room next to me
who like playing video games. Very noisy video
games."

"Ah. Now I see." He reached across her to pick
up the first page of the grant instructions and his
arm brushed against hers.

She wanted to gnash her teeth.

She hadn't succeeded that day with Squire
Clay.

She'd failed to find a dress at Classic Charms,
because when she'd gone by, the small store had
been closed for the day.

And now, when she needed to be entirely focused on the grant-writing task at hand, all she
was able to focus on was him.

She had only a couple of hours before the library closed, and she needed to make the most of

them. Midnight was going to arrive in five hours whether she was prepared or not.

Doing her best to ignore Archer, she pulled out a fresh sheet of paper and clicked her pen a few times. She pondered for a while, then wrote out her first sentence, which was simple and straight-forward.

Weaver needs a new library.

She scratched it out, tossed down her pen and gave him an annoyed look. "What *are* you doing here?"

"Lawyers need libraries like flowers need rain."

She rolled her eyes. "You have a more than adequate library in your own house. You showed it to me last night."

He smiled slightly and brushed a lock of her hair away from her cheek. "Caught me. I was over at the sheriff's department. Saw your car parked here when I was leaving."

"So?"

"So, I thought I'd see how things were coming along."

"Nothing's changed since the last time you saw me. I haven't managed to raise the rest of the money we need."

He looked amused. "That would have been quite the accomplishment if you had. Vivian would feel compelled to give you a raise in pay."

"I also haven't gotten Squire Clay to agree to attend Vivian's cocktail party tomorrow. He's the last holdout on the council."

"Yeah, well, that's not surprising, either. Lot of murky water under that particular bridge."

She raised her eyebrows, waiting, but he didn't elaborate. Instead, he angled his head as he read through the second page of grant instructions.

If she didn't get to it, not only would the library close right around her ears, but she'd end up missing the deadline.

She picked up her pen again. "Weaver needs a new library," she wrote again.

She scratched out the second, identical line, which had only served to prove how singularly unimaginative she was.

Archer's fingers brushed hers as he slid the pen from her hand. "I'll help."

She stared. But then reason intruded. Of course he'd help. It wasn't Nell herself who'd prompted his offer. The library project was spearheaded by his grandmother.

And it wasn't smart to look a gift horse in the mouth whether or not her self-protective instincts urged her to keep him at arm's length. "Do you know anything about writing a grant proposal?"

"No. But I know Lincoln Swift at Swift Oil." He gave her a quick grin as he tossed aside her pen and crumpled her carefully highlighted pages

into a ball. He nudged her chin when she opened
her mouth in protest. "Don't say anything you'll
live to regret."

"But—"

"My sister Maddie is married to him."

She blinked. And then she closed her mouth
and quickly began stuffing all of her materials
right back into the binder.

Chapter Nine

"Thank you *so* much. I can't tell you how much I appreciate your support."

Archer watched Nell pump Linc's hand and hid a smile. The only times he'd ever seen his imperturbable brother-in-law perturbed had been when he'd been caring for his little niece Layla a few years ago when she'd been abandoned on his doorstep, when Maddie had been in labor with their own son, Liam, and now, in the face of Nell's fervent appreciation.

"I'm glad to help," Linc was saying. He managed to extract his hand from Nell's. "I wish I could just tell you that Vivian's project could receive Swift Oil's grant, but I'm married to one of her granddaughters. That automatically excludes her project from consideration. But that doesn't have to stop me from putting the screws to my business associates who aren't related to her. They can dig deeper into their pockets, too."

They were at the stately house located squarely in the middle of Braden where Linc and Maddie lived. Only Maddie—who was a social worker with family services—had been called out on some emergency, which left Linc alone on Liam duty.

"Any and all support is really appreciated." Nell was beaming at Linc and it spilled over into the glance she gave Archer. He wondered if she even realized it. She'd never smiled that much when she'd worked for Pastore. "I really should have realized your connection to Vivian before now. I just—"

Linc shook his head, waving off her comment. "People who've lived here a lot longer aren't even necessarily aware. Don't worry about it." His attention perked when he heard a noise. "Just a sec." He strode from the room and returned a moment later with a cross-looking Liam in his arms.

At the sight of Archer, though, the toddler shoved at his daddy's hold, nearly launching himself into midair toward him.

Fortunately, Archer was used to the greeting

and was prepared for the catch. "Hey, bud," he said, smiling into Liam's little face. He held up his palm and Liam showed off his mouthful of stubby white teeth as he smacked his fist against Archer's hand. "Aren't you supposed to be in bed by now? It's after eight."

Linc looked chagrined. "And Maddie won't be pleased. She likes Liam down by seven."

"I know. Last time I babysat, she gave me hell for not getting him into bed on time. Said I deserved to have to watch him the morning after when he's cranky as all get-out because of it." Archer caught the bemused look on Nell's face as she watched him with the baby. "What?"

She lifted her shoulders, giving him an innocent look that he didn't buy for a second. "Nothing." She jerked back a few inches when Liam aimed his fist her way, accompanied by a stream of babble. "Just trying to imagine you babysitting."

"Hifi, hifi, hifi," Liam demanded noisily as he waved his arm again toward Nell.

"He wants you to high-five," Archer interpreted.

Her dark gaze swiveled to the baby and she lifted her palm just in time to meet Liam's next swing.

Liam chortled and squirmed in Archer's hold,

both arms outstretched as he threw his upper body toward Nell.

She looked surprised and delighted as she caught his torso, and then had to take a steadying step when she received the full brunt of the boy's weight. She quickly adjusted her grip though, and laughed into Liam's face. "Well, hello there, Liam. Aren't you a live one?" She caught his hand with hers and wriggled it. "How old are you?"

"I fi," he said giggling.

"You're *almost* two," Linc corrected wryly. "For some reason, five is his favorite word these days."

"You coory," Liam told her, patting her head with obvious glee. "Coory coory."

"Curly," Archer supplied.

"I am curly," Nell agreed. She touched Liam's smooth hair. "Is your hair curly?"

His forehead puckered. He shook his head. "No, I a boy."

Nell laughed. She shot Archer a sparkling look that made him nearly hurt inside before looking back at his nephew. "Sometimes boys have curly hair too, you know."

"Unh-uh." Liam was certain. "Hifi." He raised his fist again and she obediently tapped her palm against it. He pumped his fists up in the air and whooped.

Nell laughed again, and rubbed her face against the boy's head.

"You're watching too many basketball games on television," Archer told Linc. "Kid's starting to sound just like you."

"Come here, pal." Linc lifted his son out of Nell's arms. "Everyone is his best friend right now," he told her.

She was smiling, something soft in her eyes. "He's darling."

"Yeah." Linc rubbed Liam's head. "I think we'll keep him." He led the way from his downstairs office into the foyer, swinging Liam upside down over his shoulders.

The toddler squealed excitedly. "Daddy!"

"That'll help get him to sleep," Archer said drily. He reached around Nell to open the door. "We need to get while the getting's good. You do not want to see Maddie when she's on a tear 'cause her firstborn isn't in bed when he's supposed to be."

"I have a few tricks to calm her down," Linc assured him.

Archer shuddered. "I need to wash out my ears now." He started to nudge Nell out the door. "That's my baby sister you're talking about."

"Hold on." Linc opened a closet door and pulled out a black box about half the size of a shoebox. "If you're heading back toward Weaver, can you drop this off with your folks? Maddie borrowed these socket wrenches from your dad."

"Sure." Archer took the box. "What'd she need them for?"

"Putting together another crib." Linc winked and darted up the stairs, bouncing Liam up and down to make him squeal even more.

Archer was aware of Nell tugging his sleeve. "We going to stand here for a while or—"

He looked down at her. "Did he just say *another* crib?"

"Yes." She pursed her lips. "Is that his way of announcing another baby?"

"Yes," Linc said from the top of the staircase. Laughter was in his face. "But keep it to yourself. Maddie wants to tell your folks this weekend." He lifted his hand and disappeared along the landing.

"Great," Archer muttered as he followed Nell out through the door. "Drop some news like that on me even though I'm doing him the favor of returning the tools?"

Nell laughed. "Stop complaining. You're thrilled with the idea of another nephew or niece. I can see it on your face."

He dropped his arm over her shoulder as they began descending the dozens of steps leading from the street up to the distinguished brick house that sat high on a hill. "It keeps Meredith from looking too closely in my direction on that score," he allowed. "And don't remind me again that I'm not getting any younger. My ego still hasn't recovered from the first time."

"Please. Your ego is steel-plated."

He chuckled. It was better than letting on that she was the only one who had ever left real dents in it.

She skipped down several more steps, her hair bouncing like springs around her shoulders. He could understand his nephew's appreciation for her hair. It was even curlier than his stepmother's was, though nowhere near as long. Meredith's wildly curling hair reached almost to her waist. Nell's—on these rare occasions when it was actually down like now—bounced around just below her shoulders.

His dad had once told him that the first thing he'd noticed about Meredith had been her hair. The second had been her happy spirit, which, considering everything Archer knew about those days, said a lot about his stepmother's ability to rise above her situation.

Nell had noticeable hair, too. But until lately— until she'd left Cheyenne, in fact—the last time Archer had seen any kind of real happiness in her spirit had been when she was in law school. When, if she weren't studying, she'd been working in a dinky off-campus bookstore that she said reminded her of the one her mother had owned.

They'd finally reached the street where his truck was parked and he set the wrenches in the back seat. She'd already climbed in before he could open her door and he sighed a little inside.

Carter Templeton had raised his kids with some hard-and-fast rules.

One: you returned anything you borrowed, especially tools and money.

Two: men took off their hats indoors and held both chairs and doors for women, regardless of whether they were two or two hundred.

Three: you protected others. The people you cared about. The people who couldn't protect themselves. Even the people who didn't realize they needed protecting.

He got behind the wheel and drove across town to his parents' house. Nell was quiet, seemingly lost in her thoughts.

"You don't mind stopping at my folks' house, do you?"

"What?" She gave him a surprised look. "Of course not. I haven't seen Meredith in—" She was shaking her head. "I don't know. Too long to remember." She was silent while he drove through an intersection. "Braden's grown a lot since I was here with Ros."

"Lot of time has passed since then. Lot of changes. Fortunately, whatever Braden doesn't have, Weaver does, and vice versa. Folks around here may not have everything they want, but they pretty much have everything they need."

"Except a sufficiently large library."

He smiled slightly. "Except that." They passed a large darkened building with boarded windows. "And that." He jabbed his thumb at the window. "Movie theater. Closed at least a year ago."

"Free access to a public library is more important than commercial access to a movie house."

"Tell that to the people spending fortunes making movies." He turned a corner. "And people around this area who have to drive to Gillette or Sheridan just to see a movie in a real theater. Would be like someone in Cheyenne having to go to Denver."

She peered out the side window. "Is that building still your uncle's pediatrics office?"

"I'm surprised you remember."

She rubbed her arm. "He had to give me a tetanus shot that summer when I cut my foot—"

"—climbing the fence at the schoolyard with Ros. I remember."

"That leaves us both surprised, then." Her voice was light.

His, not so much. "I remember a lot of things, Nell."

He felt her gaze, but she didn't say anything.

And then he was pulling up in front of his parents' house. He parked and got out, retrieving the set of wrenches from the back seat. Nell was still sitting with her door closed and he pulled it open. The interior light came on, shining over the top of her dark head like some sort of halo. "Come on."

"It's late," she started to protest. "I shouldn't—"

"—avoid Meredith and let her find out about it," he said over her words. He reached in, and ignoring the consternation on her face, unsnapped her safety belt. He gestured. "Come on."

Nell's waist tingled where his arm had grazed it and she briefly debated whether it was worth taking him to task for undoing her belt without asking.

It wasn't.

When it came to debates with Archer, she rarely won. She finally huffed, swinging her legs around so she could slide out of the truck. She couldn't explain the reluctance she felt accompanying him inside his childhood home. "You could at least warn them."

"We don't need warnings in my family."

"I'm not your family."

"No matter what's going on between the two of you lately, you might as well be Ros's family, so that counts, too."

Maybe that was the problem. Seeing Meredith Templeton would bring home all over again the pain Nell felt where Ros was concerned. "You wouldn't say that about Martin."

"That's because he gives cockroaches a bad name." Archer took her arm and tugged her up the walkway toward the house. It was the same one she'd visited all those years ago.

Just a normal house. Not overly large. Not overly small. The kind of house that was comfortable and filled with family members who squabbled and laughed and always, always loved. Being here that summer after her mother had died had been a balm for Nell's aching soul.

And she couldn't believe how choked up she felt as he reached the front door and walked right in with only a loud knock and a "hello," to announce their arrival. The hand he'd kept on her arm now caught her hand, brooking no argument as he pulled her inside the house. "I brought a guest," he said as he walked across the foyer.

"In the kitchen!" a bright, feminine voice answered, and a moment later, a familiar face popped around a doorway.

Meredith Templeton's eyes widened at the sight of Nell and her smile widened even more as she hurried toward them, bringing with her the scent of lavender and patchouli and the faint jingle of bells from the bracelet she wore around one ankle. "Nell! Well my goodness, what a delightful surprise."

Nell caught the way Meredith looked beyond

her, as if she hoped to see someone else—namely her eldest daughter—accompanying them.

If Meredith was disappointed that she didn't, she hid it well as she lifted her cheek toward Archer's kiss. "I didn't even know you were back from Denver!"

"A few days now."

"You make it so difficult to keep up with you. If it weren't for the calendar Jennifer sends me, I'd never know where to find you." She lightly swatted his shoulder and turned in a brightly colored swirl of flowing fabric. She stretched out her arms. "Honey, what a treat this is."

Before Nell knew what was happening, Meredith—several inches shorter than her—had pulled her down into a tight squeeze of a hug.

Her eyes stung. "It's good to see you, too, Mrs. Templeton."

"Don't you dare call me that." Meredith pushed her back and peered into her face. "I'd heard that you began working for Vivian. She's the only Mrs. Templeton around here. And I have to say that Cheyenne's loss is certainly Weaver's gain." She twirled on her bare foot again, skipping slightly as she hurried over to a doorway. "Carter! Put down the book and come see your son." She practically danced back to them and she wrapped her arm through Nell's. "Come into the kitchen. I'm testing out a recipe for the women's wellness expo next month."

"Beware," Carter said as he entered the room and followed them into the kitchen. "This is her third go at it. She's been trying to bake chocolate brownies without using real sugar, flour *or* chocolate."

He stood as tall as Nell remembered—and looked just as stern and formidable, particularly now that he had more gray than brown in his hair. Carter offered a glimpse into the future of Archer's looks, because their handsome faces were nearly identical. His gaze rested on Nell and there was a faint smile in his eyes. "Considering you're working for my mother, you're looking well."

"She looks better than well," Meredith chided. "She looks positively wonderful!" She let go of Nell and pulled on an oven mitt. She opened the oven door and a strong scent of chocolate wafted out even before she withdrew the pan and set it on a trivet. When she was done, she tossed her oven mitt aside.

"Now." She turned once more to the accompaniment of soft bells and the swishing skirt around her ankles. "Tell me everything that's going on in your life. How do you like working for Vivian? Is Montrose behaving himself? Where are you staying?" Her bright gaze landed on her husband. "Oh, Carter, don't you wish she could stay here?"

Carter's expression when he looked at his lively wife was a combination of indulgence, bemusement and abject adoration.

It was as wonderful a thing to witness now as it had been when Nell was a teenager. And it was one of the realities that had most nagged at Ros—the fact that her mother was so deeply happy with her new family. A new family that hadn't really included Ros no matter how often Meredith reached out.

"I think she'd get a little tired of commuting between here and Vivian's house in Weaver," Carter told his wife with the same dry tone that Archer so often used. His gaze took in Nell. "But of course you are always welcomed here. We have plenty of empty bedrooms. Only times they're used these days are when we're watching one of the grandkids."

"Which is never often enough," Meredith admitted ruefully. "And because we don't have enough of them. Did you hear me, Archer?"

"I heard. You tell me often enough." Archer's amused gaze met Nell's for a moment before he turned away and pulled open a drawer.

Feeling a little overwhelmed, Nell looked from Carter to Meredith. "That's very kind of you, but—" She shook her head. "It *would* be a long drive every day." There were other reasons why she'd never agree—their son, Archer, being chief among them—but it was by far the easiest excuse.

"Of course it would," Meredith agreed. "Archer's place is much closer to Vivian's. You could stay with him."

Nell nearly choked.

"I tried telling her that." Archer gave a helpless shrug.

The problem with that, of course, was that Nell had never known him to be helpless for a single day in his life. "I'm looking for something to rent in Weaver," she said, hoping to put an end to the topic altogether.

She hadn't actually devoted any time to the endeavor in the last few days, but then again she hadn't actually had much time to do so.

"Meanwhile, she's at the Cozy Night," Archer informed his parents. He'd pulled a fork from the drawer and shoved it closed with a little snap.

Meredith looked dismayed. Carter's brows pulled together.

"It's *fine*," Nell said quickly. "There's a really nice woman and her three boys who have the room next to me and we've grilled out together by the pool and…and everything." Yes, it was an exaggeration, but under the circumstances, she thought it was a forgivable one.

"But it's the Cozy Night," Meredith protested

weakly. "It was closed down last year because of drugs."

"And it opened up again," Carter reminded her. "All cleaned up. Unless you don't believe Ali. She's the police officer in the family. She ought to know."

"Of course I believe Ali." Meredith looked at Nell again. "But surely there's a better solution while you try to find something suitable to rent. Vivian would certainly have room—"

"She doesn't want to live at Vivian's, either," Archer said. "All those years living with Ros must have rubbed off on her. Stubborn as the day is long."

The last thing Nell wanted was to get onto the subject of Rosalind.

"I'll probably be out of the motel in a week," Nell told Meredith with an optimism that she miraculously conjured out of nowhere. "And I'm hardly ever there anyway. I appreciate your concern but truly, there's no need to worry about me." She spread her hands and smiled. "I'm a little more grown up now than I was the last time I was here. I'm used to looking after myself."

Meredith clasped one of Nell's hands in hers. "And I know you're positively brilliant. Archer has said so more than once."

Nell's cheeks warmed and she couldn't help sneaking a glance at Archer. Fortunately, he was poking the fork into the contents of the hot pan so he didn't notice.

He lifted out a little hunk of brownie, blowing on it for a moment before gingerly putting the morsel in his mouth. He swore around it and swallowed quickly before sticking his mouth right under the faucet for water.

"Archer," Meredith chided. "Manners."

"Emergency measures," he said when he'd shut off the water and straightened. His expression could have belonged to Liam when he'd high-fived. "Hotter 'n hell." He grabbed the checkered towel folded over the edge of the sink and wiped his chin. "A little sticky. But they taste pretty good."

Meredith crossed her arms. "And why do you make that sound surprising?"

His laugh was rich and full and it curled right around Nell.

He dropped a kiss on his stepmother's head. "I adore you almost as much as my old man does, but even he would agree that not all of your kitchen experiments have been towering successes."

Meredith gave her husband an equally arch look. "Is that so?"

Carter's smile was slow. He crossed the room toward her. "Do you want me to say I fell in love with you because of your baking skills?" He closed his hands over her shoulders. "Or do you want me to tell the truth and say I fell in love with you for your—"

Meredith raised her hand. "That's enough," she warned with a musical laugh. But then she went up on her toes and caught his face between her hands, pressing her lips to his.

The kiss didn't last long. It wasn't some display of crazy-hot passion.

But the sheer intimacy in the look that passed between Meredith and Carter made Nell ache inside.

This. The word whispered through her. *This is what it should all be about.*

She found her eyes sliding toward Archer.

He'd hooked open the refrigerator door and was pulling out the milk jug. He poured himself a small glassful, sent an inquiring look Nell's way, and at her bemused headshake, returned the jar to the refrigerator. Then he scooped up another forkful of brownie and, this time, chased it with the cold milk.

"Definitely better," he said. "But if they don't have real sugar or flour in them, what do they have?"

"I've learned it's better not to ask these things," Carter cautioned humorously. He'd circled his arms around his wife's shoulders, holding her loosely against his chest. "Thought I'd taught you that, as well."

"You know me." Archer's gaze landed on Nell's face. "I like living dangerously."

Meredith's eyes sparkled with merriment above her husband's forearms as she looked toward Nell. "What are we going to do with these men?"

Nell managed a smile that she didn't feel. Neither of these men—Archer in particular—was hers with which to do anything. "You said you're preparing for a women's event?"

"I am, indeed." Meredith ducked out from Carter's embrace to begin cutting the brownies and scooping them onto a plate. "I'm very excited about it. Thanks to Vivian's financial support, we'll be able to bring in a few national speakers. We'll have free health screenings, a mobile mammogram truck, yoga sessions, art sessions, cooking, child care naturally. All sorts of things. It's a first, of course, but I'm hoping that it'll be successful and we can repeat it every year."

"Sounds great. If there's anything I can do to help—"

"Bless you, sweetie. There's always room for help." Meredith suddenly looked at Archer. "I bet she could help with your session, honey." Her head swiveled back toward Nell. "He's giving a workshop on navigating the legal system when it comes to child custody issues and child support." She clasped her hands, actually rising up on her bare toes in her enthusiasm. "It would be perfect! Women are often more comfortable talking to another woman about some things. Archer, you know that. You've talked about it so often. The two of you could be partners. Work as a team."

Archer's inquiring gaze caught Nell's and held it. "Well? What do you say? Do you finally want to be my partner?"

Her mouth turned dry.

He'd asked her that once. To be his partner.

It had been shortly after they'd slept together.

Shortly after Ros—who hadn't even known about her stepbrother and her best friend—had told Nell about the latest fling Archer was having with one of their professors.

Nell had been a month from graduating. She'd still needed to pass the bar exam.

She'd needed to remember that following her head never hurt the way trusting with her heart had.

She'd turned him down.

And chosen Martin instead. Martin, who'd been a mentor. Martin, whom Nell owed for having kept a roof over her head. Martin, whose approval Nell had wanted almost as badly as Ros had wanted his love.

"Yes," she said. Her head felt a little dizzy. As if she really were spiraling down into Archer's green, green gaze. "I'll be your partner."

Meredith clapped her hands happily and the

sound seemed to echo inside the warm, inviting kitchen.

Or maybe it was just inside Nell's head.

"This'll be *just* perfect," the older woman was exclaiming. "The two of you together? You know exactly what you're getting."

But now that Nell had agreed, and she realized that deviltry had entered Archer's eyes, she wasn't sure at all what exactly she'd be getting.

Chapter Ten

Meredith insisted they celebrate the decision with more brownies and coffee.

The coffee was welcome. Particularly when the sticky brownies dried out and turned hard just as soon as they were fully cooled and needed something to help wash them down.

It was close to midnight when Archer finally managed to get them out the door and on the road back to Weaver.

"Sorry about that," he said once they were actually driving away from the house.

Nell hugged her to-go cup that Meredith had sent with them. The hot coffee it contained was sweet and light, exactly as Nell liked. "About what? Getting saddled with me for your workshop at the women's expo?"

"If you didn't want to do it, you could have said so."

"I didn't say I didn't want to do it. I said *you*—" She broke off, shaking her head and looking out the window. "Never mind."

"Nobody saddled me with you. Not even Meredith. She had a good idea and I agreed with her. So are we partners or not?"

He was the one who sounded annoyed.

She decided pointing it out was not a smart route to take. "Yes," she said. "We're partners." Then she looked out the window beside her because the words sounded far more momentous than they ought to when all they were talking about was a simple workshop. The kind of workshop she'd conducted more than once for Sally Youngblood at the legal aid office.

She nervously rubbed her finger up and down the side of her warm cup as the lights of Braden thinned.

Just a workshop. Just a workshop.

Just. A. Workshop.

Finally, when the lights behind them had fallen away altogether, she felt brave enough to tackle the lingering sense that there was something amiss. "We were still talking about the women's expo, right? The workshop."

He waited a beat. Long enough for the skin on the back of her neck to prickle.

A lot.

Then it was just one word from him. "Sure."

She was not reassured.

But it wasn't as if he could commandeer her into becoming a real partner. She had a job now, anyway, working for his grandmother. At least temporarily until the library was truly underway.

And what are you going to do then?

There were so many thoughts circling in her mind, it was exhausting. She was glad she wasn't the one behind the wheel. Until she'd driven with Archer to see Lincoln Swift earlier that evening, she hadn't realized how the road became even narrower and more winding on the way to Braden once it passed where Archer lived. Considering how distracted her thoughts were, she'd be a danger on the road.

"Thanks for bringing me." She meant it, but mostly she needed to hush the noise inside her head. "To see your brother-in-law, I mean." Seeing Lincoln had been the purpose for the trip, but that seemed to have taken a back seat once Archer had pulled her inside his parents' home. "It was really nice seeing your folks again, too. It doesn't seem like they've changed a bit. They're so—" She broke off, hunting for the right words.

He seemed to understand, though. "I know. They fit. You look at them and you think, *this*."

She shivered and all of the busyness inside her mind went still.

This.

He shifted slightly in his seat and if he noticed her startled reaction, he didn't show it.

"If you had to pick two people who seem ideal for each other, you'd never think to pair a guy like my dad with a woman like Meredith. He's rules and order and always hedging against disaster. The only thing orderly about Meredith is her constant disorderliness. But together, they're like two halves of a whole."

He dropped his right hand down to his own to-go cup on the console between them.

Nell knew the contents would be the exact opposite of hers.

She rested her head against her backrest and studied him. His profile was little more than a shadowy outline. Not even the bluish glow from the gauges on his dashboard was enough to penetrate the utter darkness.

She could look her fill and he'd never be the wiser.

She fit her coffee cup into the holder molded into the console. She was very aware of his arm just a few inches away from hers. If she spread her fingers, they'd be touching his. "Ros always saw that, too. The way her mom and your dad were together."

"It's part of the reason why she didn't like having to come and visit."

"You knew?"

"Hard not to. Through no fault of her own, she got the short end of the stick."

She felt indignant on behalf of her friend who no longer even wanted to *be* her friend. "If you feel that way, why have you always been so at odds with her?"

"Calm down, Cornelia. Understanding her situation doesn't mean she wasn't a pain in the butt." He let out half a laugh. "Even under the best of circumstances, Ros is competitive as all hell." She felt his gaze. "Tell me I'm wrong."

She couldn't. Her indignation was dribbling away. "There's nothing wrong with having a competitive streak, though." Ingrained habit still made her defend Ros. "It makes us all strive to do better."

"Some people strive to do better just because they want to do better. Not because their life seems to depend on outrunning the person in the lane next to them." He lifted his cup for a drink and when he lowered it once more, his arm seemed to be resting even closer to hers. "Problem with Ros is that she's never understood she didn't have to compete for Meredith's love. She was always so busy trying to outrun us all that she couldn't see she was also running in the wrong direction. You know why Meredith left Martin?"

The abrupt question took her by surprise. She moistened her lips, feeling suddenly awkward. "Not, um, not really."

"For a lawyer, you're a crappy liar."

"I'll take that as a compliment since I don't have any desire to be a really good one!"

"You heard that she was having an affair with my dad when they worked in the same office. That's why you think they split up."

"It's none of my business!" She wished they'd never ended up on the subject. Meredith held a secretly special place in Nell's heart. She had done so ever since that long-ago summer. Whatever her history was, Nell had no intention of sitting in judgment.

"Martin beat her."

"What?" Shock slid through her with nauseating speed. "How do you know?"

"Because my dad had the pictures he took of her when he first realized what was happening."

Archer looked toward her, as if he expected her to say something, but she was too busy struggling with her dismay and after a moment, he turned his attention back to the road. "Ros was just a baby then," he went on. "When Dad first left the army, he moved with Hayley and me to Cheyenne. He went to work at the insurance company where Meredith was working part-time as a file clerk. That's how they met."

"If Martin was abusing her, how did he ever end up with custody of Ros? How—"

Archer closed his hand over her fingers and her words stuck in her throat as surely as Meredith's everything-free brownies. Nell would've reached for her coffee to wash the knot down but doing that meant moving her hand from beneath his.

"You know the position of authority an abuser holds over his victim," Archer's voice was neutral. "She was afraid."

Despite the neutral tone, though, Nell could tell there was a volcano brewing beneath the surface.

She'd never seen Archer truly angry. Over the years, in court and out, she'd seen him hypnotically charming. Contemptuously cold. And myriad shades in between.

But she wasn't sure she'd ever actually seen him angry. Really and truly, wrenchingly angry.

She wasn't sure she ever wanted to see that.

"Afraid," he repeated, squeezing her fingers tighter. "And more afraid than ever once my dad got involved."

She shifted in her seat, angling toward him even more. "Archer, you don't have to—"

But clearly he did, because he ignored her tentative attempt to stop him. "He started out just wanting to help her escape her situation. It hadn't been that long since *my* mom had died. Hayley was like three years old."

Nell felt his gaze slide her way again even though she couldn't actually see it.

"He tried talking Meredith into leaving Martin—for her own sake if nothing else—but she refused. She'd already tried to escape once and the slimeball had her convinced that she'd never see Ros again if she tried leaving him."

Nell couldn't stop a dismayed sound from leaking out. Even if she hadn't discovered his attempted collusion in the Lambert probate matter, Nell could well imagine Martin convincing Meredith of such a claim. He simply was that intimidating.

Nell knew Meredith didn't have other family. More than thirty years ago, she would have been so young. So alone.

"No wonder you can't stand him."

"That's just the start." The neutrality of Archer's tone edged into grimness. "Even though he now knew the truth, my dad couldn't stop Meredith from quitting her job. He couldn't force her to leave her husband. She doesn't talk about what happened during those few years that followed, but you can be pretty certain Martin didn't change *his* ways. People like him usually don't."

"No. They just get more entrenched in them."

Archer's fingers squeezed hers. "Anyway, Dad moved us to Braden. I don't know if it was because he wanted to put more distance between him and Meredith or not. My uncle was already there with his medical practice. So maybe it really was because of that. In any case, he started up his own agency and time passed. But eventually he ran into Meredith again. And this time, things got even more serious even faster, and she ended up pregnant with the triplets. Which put her really between a rock and a hard place. Protect herself and the babies she was carrying by leaving to be with my father, or stay with Rosalind, who was still just a toddler."

Nell pressed her lips together. Even though she knew how that situation had ultimately ended, she couldn't help feeling anxious. "What happened? What made her leave Ros with him?"

"She didn't leave Ros."

"But—"

"Martin discovered the affair. He tried to raise his hand against her again but this time she fought back. She ended up clocking him with a cast-iron frying pan. Knocked him out cold. Put him in the hospital, in fact, with a concussion. She bolted *with* Ros and went to my dad." Archer's voice tightened. "But a few days later, the cops came to arrest her for assault and they put Rosalind right back in her father's hands."

"But Martin was the abuser," Nell argued as if there was something that could still be done about it. "He was the one who belonged in jail. Not Meredith—"

"Use your head, Cornelia. This was more than thirty years ago. Laws then were even less perfect than they are now. You know that sometimes the bad guys win. He was already making a name for himself in legal circles. The people's champion." He made a disgusted sound. "He had people lined up vouching for his character. Attesting to what a good father he was. The best parent for Ros, certainly, since his wife was clearly unstable. How hard do you think it was for him to find a judge who gave him quick custody? Particularly with Meredith in jail for assault."

"Was there never a record of this?" It was inconceivable that Ros didn't know any of this, but if she *had* known, how much different would things have been for her friend? Ros wouldn't have worked her entire life to earn her father's love if she'd known he'd abused her mother.

"Officially?" Archer made a rough sound. "You worked with Pastore long enough to know his methods. The only records that exist show his magnanimousness in dropping the assault charges. He'd won, of course. He had Ros. And Meredith was still terrified that he'd disappear with her the way he'd threatened before. So Dad pulled out those old photos."

"He still had them!"

"Insurance," Archer explained.

"I'm surprised Meredith allowed it."

"I don't know that he gave her a chance to argue the point. But it was good that he'd kept them. Even as an abuser, Martin had been calculating. He hadn't been stupid enough to leave marks on her where a casual observer might see them, but he had been twisted enough to use a cigarette to basically brand his initials on her. The photos were pretty intimate."

Nell's stomach churned even more. She thought about the warm, loving woman experimenting with her brownies. And about Martin the last time Nell had seen him in his office. Sitting at his desk, arrogant and confident despite the evidence she'd all but thrown into his face. "That's revolting."

"It was. All along, Meredith had been adamant that the photos would never be seen. It's amazing that she'd let my dad even photograph her like that in the first place."

"She wanted help."

"Help that she ended up not even taking for another few years. But by then, she had more than just herself to consider. She was pregnant. How could she sacrifice one child to make sure the others who weren't even born yet were safe from Martin? She told me once that every step she took landed her deeper in the weeds until she felt like she was drowning in them. And that falling for my dad—right or wrong—was like finding air to breathe again."

"Thank goodness for that." Nell's eyes burned. "So what happened? I assume your dad used the threat of exposing the photos as leverage against Martin."

"Let's just say they came to an agreement."

"Martin had to keep Ros in the state where Meredith would have reasonable visitation," Nell concluded.

"He also had to get the assault charges dropped. And if he ever laid a hand on Ros the way he did Meredith—" He shook his head. "I think my dad would have ended up in jail for attempted murder."

"But once Martin was over the barrel, why not push for regaining custody altogether?"

"Because even when he's over a barrel, he has an angle. Meredith and Dad weren't the only ones who could go public. Martin could, too. Those photos were a double-edged sword. As much proof of their affair—remember, they'd been taken a few years earlier, even—as they were proof of Martin's abuse."

"Of course he had an angle," she said huskily. He'd had one with *her*, and she was chopped liver in the scheme of things.

"Meredith didn't care about her reputation, but she did care about Dad's. He had a new insurance business where reputations did matter. She didn't want any of her children exposed to Martin's vitriol. You know him. He would've made sure the scandal never died. And my dad didn't want Meredith to be humiliated that way, either. The scandal of it all had taken a toll on her. She'd already spent weeks in jail. He was worried about her health. About her pregnancy. So they took what they could get.

"I believe they intended to push for more at some point, but it never came to pass. Meredith never wanted Ros to know how treacherous her father had been."

Nell turned even more toward him, pulling one knee up beneath her. "But they told *you*."

"My father told me," he corrected. "Not until Meredith agreed to it first, but he was the one to tell me. And only so I could make sure Ros would always be protected where Martin was concerned in case something ever happened to them. Just because Martin never mistreated her once all the dust had settled after the divorce, it doesn't mean he wouldn't change his stripes again if he had the chance. Ros idolizes him. Always has. Does even now when she's a grown woman who should know better. But if she were to get on the wrong side of him?"

"How long have you known all this?"

"Since I passed the bar. Dad calls me up. Invites me out for a beer. Figured he was going to congratulate me. You know. All that." He shifted in his seat again, the only evidence that the subject was more disturbing than his steadily delivered explanation hinted at. "And he did congratulate me. But then he pulls out an envelope containing a half-dozen old photographs and—" He made a rough sound. "It's bad enough seeing something like that when it's a client. When it's the woman who has loved and raised you for most of your life—"

Nell turned her hand until her fingers slid through his. The glowing dials on the dashboard blurred. "Why are you telling *me* all of this? Ros is the one who needs to know the truth."

"Like she accepted whatever truth it was that had *you* moving away from Cheyenne?"

Nell's chest squeezed. Her situation with Martin was a water droplet in comparison with what he'd done to Meredith and Ros.

"As smart as she is, Ros is not reasonable when it comes to Martin. She's been drinking that Kool-Aid for too long now. Which leaves it up to someone else to keep a watch out for her interests even if she never knows it's happening."

"Yes, well, if she did, she'd be furious."

"Yes, well, chances are she won't ever know. Won't ever need to know." His fingers curled tighter around hers. "But Dad had his plan of succession by telling me. I have my plan by telling you."

She felt a sudden knot in her throat. "Archer—"

"—And I trust you enough to know you'll never breathe a word of it unless it's to protect my stepsister."

She blinked hard and looked away, but a tear still leaked from the corner of her eye, feeling just as hot crawling down her cheek as his palm felt against hers. "I don't know what to say." Her voice was husky.

"You don't have to say anything. You just have to believe what I've told you."

"You wouldn't lie about something like this." That was Martin's way. He'd twist words, twist situations. Always calculating. Always manipulating.

She stared at the console. At her hand clasped with Archer's. "Did you really want to go into practice together?" she asked suddenly. "You know. Back then. Or was it because we'd—" she swallowed and reminded herself that she was a grown woman "—because we'd slept together?"

"Yes."

She absorbed that. Then she frowned. "Yes, you wanted the partnership? Or yes, you wanted it because we'd slept together?"

"Yes," he repeated with exaggerated patience, leaving his answer still wholly unclarified.

Her breath escaped slowly. Noisily. "Obviously," she said, "you're just trying to annoy me." After taking the time to confide something so extremely personal, too. "Why?"

She realized their hands were still clasped when he rubbed his thumb across her palm. "Some habits are easier to break than others."

Then he let go of her and slowed the truck as he turned the steering wheel. A moment later she recognized the stone pillars beneath the wash of headlights.

Her nerves shot into another gear. She moistened her lips. "What are we doing here?" She was afraid of jumping to conclusions. Particularly when her thoughts were already skittering around like lines on a painting and bells were jangling inside her veins.

"It's late."

She swallowed. "So?"

"So it's been a long day and I don't want to drive any more tonight." This wasn't strictly true, since he did drive farther, at least until he reached his house where the exterior light washed invitingly down over the deck.

"Don't worry," he said as he put the truck into Park. "There are several bedrooms, including the one in the guesthouse, that you can choose from."

"I have a lot to do tomorrow," she argued, even though it was patently obvious that he wasn't going to budge. "Your grandmother's party is—"

He covered her mouth with his hand. Lightly. But the fact that he'd done it at all was enough to make her go rigid.

"Don't worry," he said in a mock whisper. "I'll take you into Weaver in the morning. Nobody'll be the wiser." He dropped his hand and shoved open his door.

She swallowed hard, watching him circle around the front of the truck. Moonlight shone down over his dark gold hair. He was so ridiculously beautiful it stole her breath. But it was the man inside who shined even brighter.

Would Ros ever know just how long he, and his father before him, had been watching out for her? Would she ever get over being kept in the dark about her father's true nature? Or would she deny the truth, even if proof were physically presented to her?

The door beside her opened.

"Well? Are you coming in or do I bring you a

blanket because you want to do something stupid like sleep in the truck?"

That, at least, spurred her to action. "I don't want to sleep in the truck," she assured him a little waspishly. What kind of prude did he think she'd become?

"All right, then." He held out his hand.

She didn't allow herself any time to think. She just took it and slid out through the door. But when she was standing firmly on the ground, she pulled her hand away and curled her fingers into her palm, holding on to the warmth that lingered.

He never needed to know. He was already leading the way up the steps of the deck.

She followed. "Which bed has the cleanest sheets?" Her voice was tart.

He turned and looked at her. "Mine."

Her foot nearly missed the next step. Her breath parked itself uncomfortably in her chest.

She peered up at him, wishing she could read his face. But he'd reached the top of the stairs and the light from the house was behind him, making his expression a wealth of impenetrable shadows. "Is that an invitation?"

"Do you want it to be?"

She felt her lips move, but no words would come. It was worse than when she'd made her first court appearance on her first real case. So many thoughts pushing inside her, all wanting to escape, and not a single one to emerge in anything remotely resembling a coherent statement.

She opened her mouth again.

A loud, yowling sound cut through the night, eclipsing the strangled sound she'd managed to emit.

She thought of bears again. Of mountain lions and who knew what else. "*What* was that?"

He chuckled suddenly as he turned and went over to the kitchen door and pulled it open. "That, sweetheart, is the cat."

Chapter Eleven

The cat?

Nell looked over her shoulder out into the night as the yowl sounded again. Plaintive. Annoyed.

"And from the sounds of it," Archer added, "he's none too happy about missing being fed."

She turned and followed him quickly into the house. "That doesn't sound like any housecat I've ever heard. Are you sure we haven't been feeding a bobcat?"

He reached into a lower cupboard and came out with a plastic bucket filled with cat food. "It's not a bobcat," he dismissed. "Go find a bedroom.

I'll be back." He brushed past her on his way out the door again.

She watched Archer from the doorway until the night swallowed him. After everything, she still felt wobbly inside.

Do you want it to be?

She hugged her arms around herself and walked out of the kitchen. Once more, that same soft light automatically came on.

She walked down the hall, passed the powder room with its pedestal sink and stopped at the staircase. His study and a small bedroom were on the other side.

The bedroom possessed a bed. Not quite as narrow as a twin, but not as wide as her overly soft bed at the Cozy Night, either.

She chewed the inside of her cheek, looking toward the room and feeling her pulse throb.

Do you want it to be?

Upstairs, there were three more bedrooms. Not including his.

Even the guesthouse had a bed. He'd told her so.

That was the best choice. The wisest choice. Don't even stay the night under the same roof.

She closed her hand over the square newel post. Placed her toe on the bottom step.

What would the cost be if she went up the rest of the steps?

She took her foot from the stair again. Walked past the staircase. But instead of going into the bedroom with the narrow bed, she turned and went into his study, instead.

Bookshelves lined three of the walls. Not just any ordinary bookshelves, either. No, these started at the floor and went all the way up to the ceiling. A dark metal rail for a rolling ladder two-thirds of the way up ran continuously around the three walls, too.

She crossed to the closest wall. Ran her palm lightly over the wildly mismatched spines. He seemed to have a little bit of everything. Biographies. Political commentaries. Science fiction. Historical fiction. Satire. Thrillers. Poetry. Even—

Her trailing fingers stopped atop the sweetly familiar name. *Julia Brewster.*

She slowly pulled out the narrow book. The glossy dust jacket was pristine. She smiled slightly as she touched the familiar rotund little penguin on the cover. "Hello, Monty," she murmured. "What are you doing here in this house?"

"Keeping company with Seuss and Dahl."

She turned on her heel, clutching the book against her chest. She felt engulfed by Archer's green, green gaze. "It's one of my mother's books."

He was still holding the bag of cat food and he

set it on the corner of his unexpectedly cluttered desk as he approached her. "*Monty the Curious Penguin.* I know."

Her chest felt tight. "But why?"

"Why not? It's your mom's first book. And it's a good one. One of Layla's favorites, in fact. She's Greer and Ryder's oldest. She'll be three in a few months and she always wants to look at the pictures when she is here."

An image of him reading to a little girl filled Nell's head way too easily. It joined the memory of him holding Liam. And it caused an increasingly familiar longing deep down inside her.

"It's not for sale anymore," she said. He'd stopped only inches away from her and she stared up at him. "It hasn't been for a very long time."

"I know. You told me."

He'd either had it for a very long time or he'd put some effort into finding it. "There were twelve in all."

"You told me that, too." His voice was impossibly gentle. "Did you ever finish tracking all of them down? You had all but one."

"The tenth." She shook her head. "Is it a coincidence? You just happen to have a copy of this?" She held up the book between them. Almost like a shield.

"Is that so hard to believe?"

"Yes." She turned and slid the book into its

narrow space on the crowded shelf, then just hovered there, her blind gaze on the myriad titles. Her heart was beating so hard, she felt dizzy.

She forced herself to turn back. To face him. Because not facing him felt cowardly. And when it came to him—to the things he'd told her tonight—the last thing she wanted to be was cowardly. Her gaze caught on his strong, angled jaw for a moment before finally reaching his gaze. "And yes, I want it to be an invitation."

"I'm sensing a *but* in there." There wasn't a single spark of deviltry in those green depths now. If there had been, she'd have been able to resist his intense lure.

Her throat tightened. Her mouth was dry. Swallowing was nearly impossible. "But I'm afraid."

His hands settled lightly on her shoulders. Thumbs roving in small, gentle…distracting… circles. "Of what?"

Of everything.

"Making another mistake," she said instead.

Something in his eyes flickered. The distracting circles slowed. Stopped. The corners of his lips lifted for such a brief moment she almost missed it. Then his hands moved. Lightly cupped her face. He lowered his head and brushed his lips across hers in a kiss as faint as a whisper.

Maybe for that reason alone, it shook her all the way down to her soul.

Then he straightened.

His hands fell away.

"We're all afraid of making mistakes, Cornelia." And he turned and left her alone in his study.

She sagged against the bookcase behind her. Against her mother's first book that was sitting on his bookshelf.

Eighteen hours later, Nell still didn't know if she'd passed up the chance of a lifetime with Archer or if she'd escaped by the skin of her teeth.

What she did know, however, was that she still felt shaky. And it was extremely inconvenient, when she ought to have all of her focus on her final checklist for Vivian's cocktail party.

Which was probably why she nearly jumped out of her skin when a young woman suddenly breezed into Vivian's office at the mansion with a cheerful "Hi! You must be Nell."

Nell stared at the gamin-faced girl. She was wearing a short, glittering red dress that showed off her legs, particularly when she hopped up to sit on the side of Vivian's desk, knocking aside a stack of mail. "Yes," Nell returned warily. "And you are—"

"Delia."

Vivian's granddaughter-slash-assistant who'd been away, Nell realized.

She suddenly felt very self-conscious in her

black dress that was nowhere near as vibrant. It didn't sparkle. It didn't cling and it covered her knees. In fact it looked more like a shapeless sack, but since Nell hadn't made it into *Classic Charms* until the last minute, she'd had to go with what had been available.

The salesgirl had insisted Nell looked *très chic*, but at that particular moment, Nell felt anything but.

"I'm Nell," she said, and quickly shook the other girl's hand. "And it's nice to meet you. Though I think we probably did meet a long time ago. I spent a summer once in Braden with your aunt and uncle. And all of you came over one day for a barbecue in the backyard. You would have been just a little girl."

Delia smiled mischievously. "Fortunately I'm not little anymore. And don't be offended when I say I don't remember you." She swung her feet that were clad in ruby-red sandals with mile-high heels. "So how do you like working for our Vivvie?"

Nell almost choked. *Vivvie* was about the last thing she'd have dared to call Vivian. But then she wasn't one of the woman's grandchildren. "It's very interesting."

She moved over to the windows to look down at the patio below. It was so nice and warm, they would be starting off out on the rear patio. Montrose had been busy in the kitchen all day making his preparations. She hoped.

All Nell could do was trust that the chef would do his part, since he'd barred everyone from entering the kitchen after having one too many shouting matches with Vivian over the menu.

There were no trays of food on the linen-draped tables. But at least the florist was there, setting out several bouquets. They were fancier than Nell thought necessary, but they weren't quite as formal and ornate as Vivian had envisioned.

Nell could only hope the decision she'd made where the flowers were concerned would be more on point than her indecision where Archer was concerned.

After spending a sleepless—and solitary—night on the narrow bed in the bedroom next to Archer's study, he'd returned her to Weaver early that morning just the way he'd promised.

With no one the wiser.

Well, nobody except Gardner, who'd been trying to get her three boys corralled and into the car for their day at summer camp.

Archer, who during the drive into town had acted as if nothing important had or had not occurred between him and Nell, had given the single mom one of his trademark smiles before driving away.

Nell marked off the floral decorations on her

checklist and wished she could mark off Archer as easily. She glanced at Delia. "Your grandmother told me she wasn't expecting you back for a few weeks."

The girl lifted a shoulder. "I decided to come home early."

Another thing that Vivian had said about Delia. She was as spontaneous as a spring breeze.

"I imagine this is usually your job." Nell gestured at the tables down below.

"Organizing one of Vivian's boring little soirées?" Delia laughed. "Not likely. She doesn't trust my taste at all. Tells me I'm too prone to sequins and glitter." She stopped next to Nell and looked out at the patio, too. "She obviously trusts yours, though. Very…tasteful."

"You mean boring," Nell interpreted drily.

"It's not boring if that's what makes you happy."

Paying exorbitant amounts of money for out-of-season floral arrangements—even scaled-down ones—wasn't something Nell cared about at all. But Vivian did.

"How many people are on the guest list, anyway?"

Nell flipped to another page in her organizer and extracted the list. She handed it to Delia. "About thirty-two. Most of the town council and their husbands and wives. A couple others. Your grandmother's architect."

"Exciting." Delia's eyes looked mischievous.

Nell raised her eyebrows. "Maybe not, but you came."

Delia shrugged. "Vivvie's not the worst pain in my side. I figure it's the least I can do. I've learned a lot from her since I started doing the personal assistant thing."

Nell looked out at the empty buffet tables again. "Did you learn how to negotiate between Vivian and Montrose?"

"That's not a skill anyone can master."

Great. Nell squelched a sigh. "Well, everything on this list is taken care of. Except for the hostess and the guests arriving. And hopefully the food will materialize."

"There will be food," Delia assured her. "Montrose might act like a total prima donna, but in the end, he'll come through for my grandmother. He always does. And there's never a problem with the guests showing up. People around here are *always* curious to get a glimpse inside the Templeton mansion."

"I can believe that." Only then did she notice that Delia was eyeing her with an assessing look. "What?"

"That dress does nothing for you," Delia said bluntly. Then she spun on her heel and disappeared as abruptly as she'd appeared in the first place.

"Gee thanks," Nell said under her breath. If she had any illusions about herself, she might have been stung. Instead, she could think only that Delia was quite the young chip off her grandmother's block. "Vivvie" was equally plainspoken.

With a few minutes on her hands, Nell left Vivian's office as well, going down the hall to her own. There was nothing else she could do to hasten Montrose short of breaking through his barred kitchen door, so she might as well make some phone calls. Try to live up to her insistence that she'd soon be moving out of the Cozy Night.

In short order, she'd made three appointments to see one of the overly expensive apartment units near Shop-World, a two-bedroom house that was over in Braden and a room in a four-bedroom house being shared by two other people.

It wasn't an impressive start, but it was still a start.

"I wondered where you'd gotten to." Once again, Delia's abrupt appearance caught Nell by surprise. She was holding two dresses hanging on hangers in one hand and she tossed them over Nell's desk. "Either one is better than that thing you're wearing. And I brought some shoes, too." She was holding a pair of black shoes by the sharp, high heels in her other hand. "Size eight?"

Nell didn't know if she was asking about her

shoe size or her dress size. Only one would be right. "Um—"

"You don't have to tell me," Delia interrupted her hemming and hawing, "but I am never wrong." Her eyes were assessing but not unkind. "And they'll go with either dress." She turned on her own high heel with a shimmering sparkle. "Leave your hair down, too," she said before she reached for the door on her way out. "You have five minutes."

Bemused, Nell looked from the door that Delia had just closed to the dresses lying in an untidy heap atop her binder and lists.

She took them by the hangers and smoothed them out, intending to just move them out of her way. But then her gaze fell on the shoes, pretty confections of narrow, velvety black straps with just a hint of sparkle on the delicate buckle.

They were pumps, all right. Closed toe, which would cover her naked, unpainted toenails, but otherwise as different from her chunky-heeled plain Janes as they could get.

And they were a size eight.

She hung the dresses on the back of the door and then kicked off her own shoes, tossing them to the corner.

Then feeling oddly trepidatious, she stepped into the black shoes and worked up the little zippers on the backs, then fastened the sparkling buckles that held the straps wrapped high around her ankles.

She straightened. She wouldn't have had a single female cell operating inside her if she'd been unable to appreciate the shoes. They were beautiful. Sexy, without being anywhere near as flashy as Delia's ruby reds.

She brushed her hands down her shapeless dress.

Then she made an impatient sound and whipped it off her head. It landed in a heap atop the shoes banished to the corner and she turned to the dresses Delia had brought. They were both black. One had spaghetti straps and a slit that went up the thigh. The other looked like a tuxedo jacket, with a softly shining satin collar and buttons that ran all the way down the front of it.

She undid the buttons and pulled the lined dress over her shoulders, certain that it would be too tight. Particularly if it had come from Delia's own closet. The younger woman was shorter and smaller.

But when Nell buttoned the first button, it fastened easily. And so did the next. And the next.

She wished she had a mirror. But even without one, she knew the front of the dress was too low cut for her plain beige bra, so she quickly pulled that off, too. She yanked the elastic band out of her hair and raked her fingers through it with one hand while she began the task of rebut-toning with the other.

She heard the door open behind her and auto-matically took a few steps away so Delia could enter. "I can't believe it fits." She was bent for-ward a little in order to reach the bottom buttons near the thigh-length hem. "When you said you're never wrong, you meant it."

"I appreciate the vote of confidence."

She whirled, then nearly tripped herself on the unfamiliarly high heels.

"Whoa there, Nelly." Archer's eyes were glint-ing as he caught her shoulders, steadying her be-fore she landed against him. His green gaze ran over her from head to toe, leaving her feeling ex-tremely flushed in all the parts in between. "Whoa there, Nelly," he repeated, a lot more softly.

Her breath felt so uneven, she might well have just run up and down a few flights of stairs. With the additional height of the heels came a brand-new vantage point on Archer's face. Her eyes were almost level with his. "I thought you were Delia."

His fingers tightened against her shoulders. "As you can see—" his gaze dropped for a moment and her lips tingled "—not so much. I recognize her influence, though. You look…different."

A warmth centered somewhere in her midriff began spreading. Upward. Downward. The lining of the dress felt cool and slick against her skin.

Her bare breasts. It wasn't a familiar sensation. But it was one worth savoring. Particularly when he was looking at her the way he was.

She moistened her lips, knowing the answer even before she asked, but wanting to hear him say it anyway. "Good different or bad different?"

"What do you think?"

She thought that not sleeping on the cleanest sheets in his house the night before was one of the biggest mistakes she'd ever made. Bigger than any mistake she'd feared she'd make by doing so.

She leaned two inches closer and pressed her mouth to his.

She felt the fast breath he drew. Felt his hands go from her shoulders, down her arms, then up her hips to her waist. Pulling her closer while memories and sensation exploded inside her cells and he angled his head, deepening the kiss that went on and on and on.

She felt his hair sliding through her fingers. Cool. Slick. Felt the brush of his cheek against hers as his head dipped and he kissed her jaw. Warm. Rasping. Felt the linen weave of his shirt when she ran her palms down his chest. Crisp. Hot.

Her head was heavy on her neck and her fingers found purchase in one of his denim belt loops as she lowered her head over him and his head dipped even farther.

He kissed the pulse raging in her throat, the valley of skin just above the low-cut first button of her borrowed dress. His hands cupped her breasts through the fabric and she couldn't stop the moan rising in her throat. A moan that was his name. "Archer."

His mouth trailed fire up to her mouth again. "Cornelia," he whispered and kissed her again and she felt his fingers tangling in her hair and her mind simply blanked out anything other than him. Other than the warmth of him. The taste. The scent. The wonderful, wonderful feel of him. Again when it had been so, so very long—

Then she felt the hard, cold surface of her desk beneath her and sanity reared its head.

Vivian's cocktail party was waiting.

She couldn't be doing this with Vivian's grandson! Not when there were probably guests already driving up to the house. When Montrose was hopefully putting aside his arrogant sneer as he showed the guests to the patio and the not-quite-ostentatious flowers and maybe, maybe some food—

"Wait, wait." Gasping, she grabbed for Archer's hands.

And realized with a start that was fueled far more by thrill than dismay that those hands were on her skin.

Her bare skin.

Her borrowed dress was gone altogether. His shirt was unbuttoned, hanging loosely off his broad shoulders, his jeans undone.

When had that happened?

"Archer," she tried again. And then gasped because his hand was sliding over her, finding her center right through her panties. She was so wet and so empty and had been for so long, that instead of reason, she embraced the insanity. She held his hand even tighter against her as she shuddered and tried to bite back her cry while his breath sounded even rougher against her ear as he urged her on.

But even as pleasure racked her, it wasn't enough.

Not giving a thought to anything else, she kicked off her panties and slid her legs along his hips, dragging him closer, wrapping her hand around him. Thrilling at the hard, pulsing heat of him.

"Now," she managed throatily. Begging. Demanding.

Either way it didn't matter, because he was there, there where she needed, pressing, filling, and she surrounded him with her legs and her arms. His mouth was open against her throat, his breath just as ragged as hers, her name just as much a groan on his lips.

"So long." His voice was a deep growl that

stroked over her nerves as surely as he stroked her so deeply inside. "Too long."

Then she was beyond hearing anything because he was at the core of the world tightening inside her, tightening until there was no more room to give and every cell she possessed exploded outward in shimmering, brilliant perfection.

Afterward, she didn't know how long she lay there on her desk, Archer's head against her breast while their panting breaths finally quieted. While the bells inside her veins stopped jangling. The cymbals in her nerves stopped crashing.

She was vaguely aware of something sharp digging into her right shoulder blade. Of an ache in her left knee where it was still hooked around him.

"I may never move again," Archer mumbled against her. But he put lie to those words by cupping her breast in one hand and running his tongue over her nipple.

The shaft of sensation streaking through her was almost painful in her satiated state and she laughed weakly. "Don't. Torture."

He braced his hands on either side of her and pushed upward. His hair was messy and falling over his brow and his bare chest bore a sheen of sweat. And his eyes, so deeply green, were almost enough to make her pull him down to her all over again.

Particularly when the corners of his lips tilted in a wicked smile. "What's a little torture?"

"This was completely unprofessional." She winced a little as she unlatched her ankles.

He dropped a kiss on the point of her shoulder. "Then it's a good thing I wasn't looking for a professional."

She found enough energy to glare at him. "Funny."

"I thought so." He straightened a little more, too, then winced himself and swore softly. "Your dorm room floor was softer than the edge of this desk." He finally straightened all the way with a faint grunt. "I may never stand straight again."

"At least you haven't been tattooed by a computer keyboard." She dragged the offending object from beneath her shoulder blade and weakly shoved it aside. It was easier to keep talking than to let the momentousness of what they'd done sink in. "And I don't recall you protesting too much." She slid off the desk, only then realizing that she was still wearing those sexy tall shoes.

His arm hooked her around the waist and he pulled her up flush against him. His gaze held her just as certainly as his arm did. "Neither did you, sweetheart."

Her fingers curled against his chest and her skin prickled. "This, uh, this doesn't change anything."

One of his eyebrows went up. "Like what?"

She felt stupid for having said it. "I don't know. But it just, you know. Doesn't." *Brilliant, Nell. Just…brilliant.*

"You'll still feed the cat, then?"

"What? Why?"

He dropped a hard, fast kiss on her lips and gave her a decidedly inappropriate swat on the behind. One that caused an equally inappropriate zip of excitement to race right through the center of her.

"I need to be in Colorado for a few weeks. Maybe longer." He hitched up his jeans and leaned over to grab his shirt off the floor. "Have a couple cases coming to a head and I need to be there."

She felt a jab of unwarranted unease. His schedule had nothing to do with her. Nor did she want it to. He was Archer Templeton, for God's sake. Just because he hadn't said a word about clients needing him in Colorado the night before when he was busy making her his "succession plan" didn't mean he was making them up. "You don't have to explain anything to me."

The look he gave her was so mild it would have alarmed her if she'd been the alarmable sort. It was the kind of look that said he knew she thought he was making excuses.

She looked away and picked up the tuxedo dress from the floor. She would have much preferred to pull on her own dress still heaped in the corner, even though it was just as shapeless now as it had been when she'd purchased it. But she couldn't. Not with him watching her. So she pushed her arms into the long sleeves once again and began buttoning that long row of buttons.

She hadn't even reached her waist when he brushed her hands aside to take over.

She damned the need that clutched at her insides when his knuckles brushed against her bare skin.

He obviously knew it, too, because he seemed to deliberately slow the task, and devilment was glinting in his eyes again. "The only reason I came here this evening was to tell you I had to leave town."

"There's this thing called a telephone."

"Yeah." He pushed through the button right below her navel. "But think of the fun we'd have missed."

She willed the wobbliness out of her knees. "Your grandmother will be disappointed. She was expecting you here for her cocktail party."

"She has you. She'll be fine."

At any other time, Nell might have appreciated his easy confidence of that fact, but it wasn't any other time.

"You going to wear your panties?"

Her skin went hot all over. "Excuse me?"

He leaned over again and when he straightened, her plain cotton panties were dangling from his finger.

She snatched them away, then balled them in her fist behind her back when the door suddenly opened and Delia stuck her head in.

She looked surprised for a moment to see her cousin there. Then speculative as her gaze bounced from Archer to Nell and back again.

"Knew the dress would fit," she said, and closed the door again.

Archer laughed softly. "Good thing she wasn't here five minutes earlier."

Nell just covered her face with her hand and wished the world would swallow her whole.

Chapter Twelve

The cocktail party was in full swing when Nell finally made it down to the patio some time later. She'd freshened up as much as she could in the powder room next to her office. She was still wearing the tuxedo dress, but at least her hair was back up in its familiar knot.

There was no sight of Delia among the people on the patio. As for Archer, he'd escaped the mansion.

As long as Delia never mentioned seeing him, his grandmother would never know that he'd been there at all.

Fortunately, Delia had been correct about

Montrose. The buffet tables were positively glorious with their artful arrangements of meats and cheeses, fruits and breads. Wine was flowing. All of the guests were smiling and soft violin music—Vivian had been strangely specific about that—was coming from the speakers built into the covered patio. In the grounds beyond the patio, lights were beginning to shimmer among the trees bordering the sea of green grass, and Rambling Mountain's peak seemed to glisten in the fading light.

As beautiful a sight as it was, Nell couldn't appreciate the mountain. Not when it reminded her of how easily she'd let Martin manipulate her. And now, after Archer's revelations, how he'd manipulated Meredith and Ros, too.

She turned away and grabbed a bottle of wine, working her way around the guests, topping off glasses as she went. Vivian, looking elegant in a gold tunic and black palazzo pants, was capably holding court.

It was still hard to believe she had any health problems at all.

Wine bottle emptied, Nell returned to the linen-draped table for another, then smiled when she saw Nick Ventura stepping through the opened glass doors between the solarium and the patio.

The sight of the tall, iron-haired man following on his heels made her eyes widen, though.

Everyone else seemed to have the same reaction at the sight of Squire Clay walking onto Vivian's patio, because all the easy chatter suddenly died, leaving only the strains of Vivaldi from the speakers and the chirp of crickets from the grounds around them.

The elderly man pulled off his dark gray cowboy hat and gave them all an irksome look. "Put your jaws back on their hinges." His gaze seemed to land on Vivian, who looked genuinely shaken.

So shaken that Nell quickly went to her. "Why don't you have a seat, Vivian." There were dozens of them—fancy ironwork things with deep custom-made cushions. And only some were actually being occupied. "I'll bring you a small plate and Nick can get started on his presentation." It was earlier than they'd planned in their timeline for the evening, but it would be a good way to distract attention away from Squire's arrival. She pulled out the nearest chair. "Right here."

"I'm not an invalid," Vivian said with enough spirit that Nell's concern dialed down a few notches. But her boss did sink onto the edge of the seat cushion a little less regally than usual. "Tell Montrose to bring me a Tom Collins."

Then she looked at Squire and waved her hand imperiously toward the vacant chair across from her. "Do you have a cocktail preference, Mr. Clay?"

"Cut the bull, Vivian," Squire said tersely. He yanked out the chair and folded his length into it. "You don't want to drink cocktails with me any more 'n I want to drink 'em with you."

Vivian gave Nell a pointed look and she quickly went in search of Montrose to prepare Vivian's drink. They hadn't planned on a full bar. Just wine and beer.

The chef was in the kitchen scooping tiny helpings of caviar onto equally tiny but elaborate edible structures. He gave her a heavy-lidded glare when she entered his domain.

"Vivian would like a Tom Collins."

He sniffed. "I'll get to it."

"Now," Nell said firmly. "Squire Clay just arrived and—"

Montrose lifted his bald head and something that might have been surprise entered his supercilious eyes. He set down the minute spoon and the tin of caviar and opened a glass-fronted cabinet filled with bottles.

A few moments later, he handed Nell a tall, slender ice-filled glass topped with a lemon twist and a cherry, and returned to his caviar task. "Now please leave," he said haughtily.

With pleasure. "Thank you for the drink," she said and left.

When she reached the patio once more, at least the two individuals seated alone together at the table no longer seemed to be quite the focus of everyone else's attention. Particularly since Nick had his presentation projecting onto the white screen Nell had arranged for that purpose.

She set the cocktail at Vivian's elbow, then moved quietly around to the buffet table.

"So." Delia appeared seemingly out of nowhere and Nell nearly dropped the two plates she'd just picked up. "Archer."

Nell flushed. She jabbed several pieces of cheese onto both plates. She kept her voice as low as Delia's. "What about him?"

"You're not his usual type."

How well Nell already knew that. "I'm not interested in being anyone's type." She quickly added meats and two small arrays of crackers. Ignoring Delia, she returned to Vivian, placing one plate near the cocktail and the other near Squire. The two didn't seem to be doing much besides glaring at each other, and Nell couldn't help wondering what had made the water under their bridge so murky.

An old romance?

That particular pairing hardly seemed likely, but what did Nell know?

She'd at least stopped wondering about it by the time Vivian's soirée finally broke up several hours later. Delia had disappeared shortly after Squire's arrival and never returned. Vivian and

Squire spent the whole time locking nonverbal horns, which had left Nell and Nick to keep the others' interest on the intended topic of the evening.

She was back in her office trying and failing not to recall what had happened there as she jotted her notes from the discussions she'd had with the guests, when Vivian found her.

Not a hair was out of place on Vivian's head, but her face looked tired and wan. "I don't know how you succeeded in getting that man here."

Nell popped out of her chair like she'd grown springs. Even though she'd exchanged the tall heels from Delia with her own dull pumps, she still stood head and shoulders above her diminutive employer. "He's a council member. You wanted the council here."

"Yes, but I still didn't expect him."

"I'm sorry."

Vivian waved her hand impatiently even though she seemed to sway a little as a result. "You did your job. Don't apologize."

Nell pushed her chair around for Vivian. "Please."

Vivian's lips thinned, but she sat. She crossed her ankles and pinned Nell with a baleful look. "Who told you? Delia? Archer? They told you about this thing squatting in my head."

Nell leaned back against the table, straightened,

then realizing Vivian was watching her closely, made herself lean back again. "Archer," she admitted.

"It's not the tumor that is making me feel old tonight," Vivian said. "It's history." She brushed an invisible speck of lint from her palazzo pants. "The worst part of getting to my age is the pallet of regret I have to haul along with me. If it weren't for my dear Arthur, that pallet would be a lot heavier. People nowadays say to live without regrets, but who actually does it? I say get rid of things that you regret while you're still young," she advised. "Life is a lot easier that way."

The edge of the table felt hard and unyielding behind Nell. But did she really regret what she'd done with Archer?

"Where was Archer this evening?" Vivian asked, almost as if she'd divined the direction of Nell's thoughts. "He knew I expected him here."

She willed away a blush. "He had to return to Colorado."

"Boy needs to settle down," Vivian murmured and pushed herself wearily to her feet. "This is quite the little hole of an office you've made. You could have chosen any other space. Outfitted it however you like." She picked up the crystal bowl full of pens. "Still can."

Nell *really* hoped that bowl wasn't precious. "I don't need a lot of space." Her job was temporary. Once the library was a reality, it would be finished.

"You'll have time to think about it." Vivian set the bowl down again. "How do you feel about your first week here?"

Like it had been so, so much longer. "I think how *you* feel about it is a little more relevant."

Vivian smiled slightly. "You accomplished something no one else has."

Nell had to step away from the edge of the table again because it felt like it was burning into her butt.

"Squire," Vivian prompted.

Nell nodded a little jerkily. "Right."

"I did his first wife a terrible wrong a very, *very* long time ago when I was married to my first husband. She was his half sister, you see. Illegitimate. Back in the day when those things mattered. Trivial, you know. You find that out when you get old." Vivian pushed the chair up to the edge of the table. "If I can finally make that right, then maybe I can finally have some peace."

Nell frowned. "I'm not sure I like the sound of that."

"Now you sound like Archer. Don't worry. I don't plan to kick the bucket any sooner than the maker plans for me. I'm *reducing* my load of regret. Not increasing it." She startled Nell when she patted her cheek. "Good night, dear."

Then she left Nell alone in her office.

Alone to think about her own regrets. And to face the fact with absolute certainty that Archer wasn't one of them.

"I need a favor."

Nell pushed up on her elbow to stare blearily at the screen of her cell phone, then she fell back against her pillow and put the phone back to her ear.

"It's two in the morning," she told Archer. Her heart was jumping around all over the place and not entirely because it was his voice on the other end.

It had been nearly three weeks since the cocktail party. Since she'd last seen him.

But his absence hadn't meant she'd been able to get him out of her thoughts. Or her fractured dreams.

And it certainly hadn't meant she hadn't talked to him on the phone. Somehow, he'd developed the art of calling her at the most inconvenient of times.

When she was stepping out of the shower in the morning.

When she was in the middle of discussing site selections for the library now that the town council had finally green-lighted the project.

When she was sound asleep in her bed while dreams of Archer danced in her head.

He called to ask about the cat. He called to talk about the workshop they'd be conducting at the wellness event. He called to check on Vivian.

"The phone rings at two o'clock in the morning and you answer it because you think something disastrous has happened," she told him, not caring at all that she sounded cross. "Not because you think someone's calling for a *favor*. I'm already feeding the danged bobcat every day for you." An inconvenience that had tempted her more than once to give up her boycott of his guesthouse. Particularly since she still hadn't found better lodgings than the Cozy Night, where she didn't even have the engaging Gardner and her three boys next door anymore. They'd packed up earlier that week to head onward to whatever it was that had been calling them ever farther away from their Ohio origins. "What more do you want?"

He laughed softly. "Dangerous question, Cornelia."

She covered her eyes with her arm. She still couldn't blot out the image of him, sweating and breathless, moving against her.

It had been the main feature of the dream her ringing phone had interrupted, and her insides still felt shaky and hollow.

"What's the favor?"

"Judge Fernandez called for a status meeting for tomorrow morning for a client of mine. I'm still here in Denver. Have court all day and I'm not going to be able to make it. Need you to stand in for me. Should only take a few minutes."

Judge Fernandez was the judge who'd handled the Lambert estate.

Nell dropped her arm and stared up at the dark ceiling. Regrets, she thought.

Ever since the night of the cocktail party, the memory of Vivian talking about dragging around her pile of regrets had been haunting her.

"What time?" she asked resignedly.

"Nine o'clock in the judge's chambers."

"Client?"

"Matt Rasmussen. Drunk and Disorderly ninety days ago. Third one. He's been attending cessation meetings twice a week. Walking the good walk. He'll meet you at the courthouse."

"Fine." She waited a beat. "Anything else? Any briefs you need me to write for you, too?"

His laugh was soft in her ear. "Good night, Cornelia."

She muttered a cranky good-night back to him and swiped her phone silent. But she still could feel the smile tugging at her lips as she buried her face in her pillow once more, and she wondered if he'd be calling again in a few more hours, catching her naked and wet from her shower.

But her phone stayed silent.

And at 9:00 a.m. the next morning, she walked into Judge Fernandez's chambers alongside Archer's middle-aged client.

A few minutes later, after having reported on his progress in the last month, Matt Rasmussen walked out again.

But Nell stayed.

She reported everything that had occurred with the Lambert estate. She didn't spare one word, not even her own culpability for failing to report everything the moment she'd discovered it at the beginning of the summer—a cause for censure in and of itself.

It took hours. It took Judge Fernandez calling in a court reporter to get everything on record, and conferencing in members of the Professional Responsibility Board to figure out exactly how to proceed with Nell's complaints against Martin Pastore.

When Nell walked out again, she didn't know if she'd ever practice law again, but she did know that even if she didn't—even if Martin were able to wiggle out of this and succeeded in putting all the blame on Nell's shoulders the way he'd planned—she'd done the right thing.

It wasn't a cast-iron skillet upside his head.

But it was close enough, and her only regret

about anything was that Ros might once again be hurt in the fallout.

She might have been drawn into Archer's whole succession plan business, but that didn't necessarily mean she agreed with it. Ros should have had the opportunity to know just how hard her mother had fought to keep her.

But Meredith's secrets weren't Nell's to tell, either.

She could deal only with her own, and she was glad to have all of it off her chest once and for all.

Those particular chips would fall as they may.

The courthouse was near Ruby's, and even though it was nearing closing time for the diner, Nell went inside and slipped onto one of the round stools at the empty counter and returned Tina's wave. She was suddenly famished in a way she hadn't felt in a long time.

She was halfway through her meat loaf sandwich and hot fudge sundae chaser when Delia appeared. She had a *Classic Charms* shopping bag over her arm and she dumped it on the counter as she took the stool next to her. "Montrose told me you took the day off."

Nell dabbed her cheek with her napkin and it came away with a smudge of sticky chocolate. "Was handling some court business. What'd you buy today?" Since Delia's return to Vivian's, Nell had gotten used to the younger woman's penchant for shopping.

Delia reached in the bag and pulled out a navy blue sundress patterned with bright yellow polka dots. "I got it to wear to Meredith's wellness event. Cute, huh?" She didn't wait for Nell's nod before dropping the dress back into the bag. "He's afraid you're looking for another job."

"Who?"

"Montrose."

Nell stared. "He hates me."

"He hates everyone. But he is still afraid you're planning to leave."

"He told you that?"

"Oh, God no. But I can still tell."

Nell smiled wryly. "How? The same way you can tell what dress size someone takes?"

"Hey, don't knock my one skill."

"You've got more than one skill," Nell chided.

"Not according to some people." Delia folded her arms atop the counter, not looking unduly concerned by that declaration. She pinched one of the French fries from Nell's plate and gave her a sidelong look. "Heard from Archer lately?"

Nell's nerves gave a reflexive little twitch. She wasn't likely to forget that Delia had nearly caught Nell and Archer together. "This morning. Part of the court business."

"The two of you go way back, don't you?"

Nell hesitated. "Sort of. We've known each other a long time. More than twenty years when it comes right down to it. Why?"

"Was it always?" Delia waggled her hand in the air. "You know. Like that with him?"

Nell polished off the rest of her sandwich, eyeing Delia more closely. She swallowed and wiped her lips with the napkin again. "Like what?"

Delia huffed. She rolled her eyes. "Were you always hot for each other?"

Nell was glad she'd swallowed or she would have choked. "Not when I was fourteen," she assured. "My mother had just died."

Delia frowned, quick sympathy entering her eyes. "How awful."

"It was. But I had my best friend. And a summer with your aunt Meredith. It helped." She reached over the counter to grab a clean spoon, then nudged her partially finished sundae toward Delia. She handed her the spoon. "Want to tell me what's really on your mind?"

Delia took the spoon and jabbed it into the melting ice cream. "Archer tell you I'm the screwup of the Templeton clan?"

"Of course not!"

Delia slowly sucked the ice cream off her spoon. "My brother's an honest-to-goodness air force hero. My sister is a doctor. Only thing I can do is guess other women's dress and shoe sizes."

"You've been Vivian's personal assistant for the last few years."

"You know Vivvie well enough by now to know she doesn't need a personal assistant. She figures out little tasks to keep me busy so I can earn a paycheck from her, which—despite the source—makes my dad happy. Which, in turn makes her feel better about the crappy childhood he had."

"I think you're underestimating yourself." Nell sucked on her own spoonful of ice cream. "So who's the guy?"

Delia grimaced. She dropped her spoon on the counter with a little clatter. "Nick."

"Nick?" Nell was a little slow. "You mean Nick *Ventura*? Isn't he—"

"Younger than me?" Delia nodded. "Four years."

"That's not the end of the world. What's four years?"

"He already has a master's degree." She propped her chin on her hand. "I'm a thirty-year-old with a high school degree." She twirled a finger in the air. "Whoopee."

"If you want more, go back to school."

"I don't want more," Delia said. "That's the problem. The idea of going back to school?" She shuddered dramatically.

"What about him? Does he know you're interested in him?"

Delia's lips twisted. "Unless he's been living under a rock. Which he has not." She suddenly twirled around on her stool, pressing her back to the counter and stretching out her legs. She was wearing shorts and a clinging T-shirt and could have easily passed for someone much younger than Nick Ventura. "So how serious is it with you and Arch?"

Nell automatically shook her head. "Archer's never serious about anyone."

"That's not exactly what I asked."

"It's not serious."

Delia didn't look convinced, but at least she dropped it and picked up her spoon again, and together, the two of them polished off the rest of the hot fudge and ice cream.

When they left the diner, they went their separate ways. Delia presumably headed back to Vivian's, where she occupied two rooms in what she lightly referred to as the West Wing.

Nell, though, headed out to look at another house for rent that had shown up the day before on the bulletin board at Ruby's. After having looked at more than a dozen potential places in the past three weeks, she wasn't holding out much hope.

Perhaps her lack of hope was the missing ingredient, though, because the small bungalow located not far from the Cozy Night was very nearly perfect. Oh, it needed a good scouring inside and out and the kitchen was ancient. But that still wasn't a deterrent for Nell. It wasn't as if she'd been gaining any new kitchen skills staying at the Cozy Night for the past month. The rental had two bedrooms, one bathroom that was slightly less ancient than the kitchen and an overgrown yard.

And it meant she could finally get the rest of her belongings out of the storage unit in Cheyenne.

She wrote a check covering the deposit and the first month's rent right there on the spot. She called around to the contacts that she'd been making since coming to town until she had a landscaper who could come and clear the yard the following afternoon and a cleaning crew who could be there even sooner.

She felt so energized by her progress that she went back to the motel and told the kid at the front desk—they were ever changing so Nell had never managed to learn any of their names—that she'd be checking out in the morning.

Then she filled the tank in her car with gas and, armed with an enormous cup of hot coffee in her console, she set off for the storage rental place in Cheyenne. By the time she rolled into town several hours later, her stomach was growling again and she stopped at a fast-food place for some dinner not far from Archer's house.

It had been only a couple of months since she'd woken up in his guest room bed there, but it felt like it was so much longer.

With both her stomach and her coffee mug refilled and knowing he was in Denver anyway, she turned down his block and trolled down his neat and tidy street. It was such a wildly different setting than his house outside Weaver and she wondered how much more different his apartment in Denver would be.

She'd never before considered that she might actually want to see it one day.

It was still light enough outside not to need the streetlights but inside houses up and down the street, lamps were beginning to come on in front windows and porch lights were beginning to come on by front doors. His house was no different. Golden light gleamed from the fixtures on either side of his front door, spilling down over the brick steps, and she smiled slightly because it was such a homey, charming sight.

When she saw a shadow move across one of the mullioned windows, she thought she'd imagined it. But when it happened again, she pulled right over to the curb and parked. She grabbed her cell phone and swiped the screen. Pressing the listing for her most recent calls, she heard clicks and a faint whir before it rang. Once. Twice. Three times.

His deep voice answered, and her stomach dipped, but it was just his voice mail message. "This is Archer Templeton, attorney at law. Leave a message. If it's an emergency, contact my office at—"

She peered through her windshield at his house, watching for another glimpse of someone inside while his voice reeled off his business numbers. "It's Nell," she said after the beep. "I'm in Cheyenne to empty my storage unit. Do you have someone staying at your house?" Then she hung up.

Crime wasn't exactly rampant in the town. But Archer, despite porch lights, was often gone for long stretches at a time. She waited for him to call for an interminable ten minutes, and when he didn't, she just exhaled and turned off the car engine. She crossed the street and skipped up the steps and walked across the porch, peering in through the front window.

The curtain panels on the inside were sheerer than she expected and easily afforded her a view of the woman standing near the fireplace.

Judge Taylor Potts.

And the man sprawled comfortably in his overstuffed chair. She could even see the cell phone clasped lightly in Archer's broad, long-fingered hand.

She jerked back but not quickly enough to miss

Taylor moving across the room to sit on the arm of his chair. To close her hand over his arm and lean closer to him.

Nell turned on her heel and darted down the steps. She raced across the yard. The street. Practically threw herself into her front seat and fumbled the car key into the ignition.

A moment later she roared down the block and around the corner, barely having the presence of mind to slow down because she was in a residential zone and the last thing she needed was a speeding ticket.

He'd told her he was still in Denver. That he had court all day.

Her fingers strangled her steering wheel as she drove to the storage unit. She should have known better. The man didn't make promises. He just kept moving on, routinely changing one woman on his arm with the next.

Never leaving anyone behind with hard feelings.

Except her.

Chapter Thirteen

"I've been leaving you messages for over a week."

Nell gave Archer a baleful look and turned away from him. She pointed accusingly at Montrose. "You said you'd warn me if he showed up."

His grandmother's chef and majordomo, wearing a white apron over his black suit, actually looked abashed.

It was unsettling enough that Archer felt mildly sorry for the way he'd bullied his way past the man when he'd opened the door at the small house where Nell had moved.

It had taken him a few days before he'd even been able to track down her address. It had been easy enough to find out that she'd moved out of the Cozy Night.

Not so easy to locate where she'd gone after that, particularly when his grandmother had abruptly departed for Philadelphia and taken Delia with her. Aside from his cousin promising him that it wasn't for health reasons and confirming that Nell *was* still in charge of the library project, he'd gotten no more information from that quarter.

Between Gage needing him to deal with Noah's latest situation and his caseload in Denver, he'd actually resorted to assigning Jennifer to the task of discovering Nell's whereabouts.

It shouldn't have been so hard in a small town like Weaver, but Nell wasn't exactly known for her talkative nature when it came to her personal business.

The way she'd kept quiet about Martin and the Lambert estate was a perfect example of that.

And now, the fact that Montrose was at Nell's at all was just one more reason why Archer felt like he'd landed in some alternate universe.

He followed her from the small kitchen where a pile of dough and flour was covering the only counter and out into a small, fenced yard. A rickety-looking picnic table was partially covered with a bag of potting soil and several plastic pots.

Even Nell looked different. She was wearing a sleeveless purple-and-green tie-dyed dress that looked as if it could have come right out of his bohemian stepmother's closet. The knit fit her as closely as a T-shirt, and when he realized he was focusing a little too hard on the swell of her breasts pushing against the fabric, he finally managed to look elsewhere. "You want to tell me what the hell is going on around here?"

She gave him a thin-lipped stare. "I don't know what you mean."

He spread his arms, encompassing the entire alternate universe around them. "You've been avoiding me for days and now...all this?"

"I haven't been avoiding you." She grabbed a spade and jabbed it into the bag of soil.

He snorted. "What do you call it, then? I've been trying to reach you since I heard about the ethics complaint you filed against Martin. And what is *Montrose* doing here?"

"Teaching me how to make bread," she said as if it should be obvious. She tossed down the spade in favor of crossing her arms over her chest, which plumped her breasts even more. "The real question is why are *you* here?"

He rubbed his forehead, trying to rid the feel and taste of those breasts from his memory, and paced around the cluttered table.

The fenced yard wasn't large. She had room for the rectangular picnic table and benches, a folding lawn chair—the lounge kind—and the stack of books that sat on the grass beside it. On the other side of the small square of grass was an ancient garage. The door was open and her car was parked inside it. "Where else do you think I should be?"

"I don't know. Maybe with Judge Potts."

He spread his palms. "Why would I be with her?"

Her expression tightened even more. "You were with her last week." Her voice was flat. "In Cheyenne when you told me you were in Denver, so you tell me."

He'd been in Cheyenne to talk to the governor about Noah Locke when he'd gotten a message from Taylor. "The only conversation I've had with Taylor Potts has been about *you*."

"She was at your house," Nell said in a flat tone. "I left you a message that I thought someone was there, but that someone was you! The two of you."

"Yeah, okay, so what?" In his present mood, he'd be damned if he'd tell her what he'd gone to the house to retrieve. Meeting Taylor there, too, so she could fill him in about the ethics case had been expedient. "You saw a conversation?"

"You told me you were in *Denver*!"

"When I called you that morning, I *was* in Denver," he shot back in a clipped tone. It wasn't often that he lost his temper but he was in danger of it now. He didn't like being accused of being a liar. "I had to go to Cheyenne because of a client."

"Right."

"Don't act like I'm the one who's been withholding information. I knew you didn't leave Pastore Legal because you hadn't made partner," he said. "But at first I figured it was your business. Same as whatever the hell caused your falling-out with Ros. Only thing I knew for certain was that Martin had to be at the center of it. He's the only thing she'd hold inviolate, even above your friendship."

He circled around her and her flinch as he got nearer added a finely honed edge to the mood that had been building in him for days now.

Ever since she failed to return the first message he'd left for her.

"But after everything I told you about Meredith, after everything that happened in your office at Viv's the night of her cocktail party—"

Her dark brown eyes darted to his, then she looked away just as quickly. But she looked as wounded as he felt.

"—after *everything*," he said through his teeth, "you still didn't give me one damn hint about Pastore's collusion. I had to learn it from Taylor. And now—" he spread his arms again "—now, you're finally out of that godforsaken motel and you come here!"

"Where else would I go?"

Archer was at his wit's end, and his voice rose, too. *"To me!"*

Her face went pale. "I don't understand."

"And you never have," he said, feeling a harsh pinch inside his gut. "You won't need anybody. You obviously don't trust me."

"I—" Her lips slammed shut at the look he gave her.

"Even all this." He flicked the bag of soil and one of the plastic pots tumbled off the table. "What is all this about? Cornelia Brewster 2.0?"

Color flagged her cheeks. "What if it is? I can't practice law right now even if I wanted to. Not until the state bar decides whether or not to censure me. Your grandmother's library is just a stop-gap and one that's not even going to last all that much longer now that we've gotten the official go-ahead. For all of my adult life the only thing I have focused on is the law. I'm thirty-six years old. Isn't it about time I figured out if there's something else I might like to do?"

"For God's sake, Nell. Go work in a bloody bookstore. Or open one of your own. It's what you've *always* wanted to do. Or have you forgotten telling me that when you were a month away from graduating law school?"

She stared at him. Color rose in her face, then drained away just as abruptly. She suddenly pushed past him, bolting into the house. He hadn't taken two steps into the kitchen after her when he could hear the sound of her retching through the thin walls.

He shot Montrose a look. The man was sitting at the table, looking like he wished he were anywhere else. "Suddenly Nell's your best friend?"

"She doesn't take advantage of Mrs. Templeton," he said in his annoyingly pompous way.

Archer raked back his hair. "She doesn't take advantage of anyone," he muttered. "Has she been sick like this before?"

Montrose's lips pursed. Obviously he wasn't going to say.

Which actually said all that Archer needed to know.

Annoyed with the chef, annoyed with her and most of all annoyed with himself, he went to find her.

She was sitting on the floor of a bathroom smaller than a coat closet, resting her head on her knees. Her curly hair looked darker than ever splayed across her pale shoulders.

He had five sisters. Four of whom had babies.

"Are you pregnant?"

Her head whipped up. Her eyes were like saucers of hot fudge. Glistening. Brown. "Don't be ridiculous."

He flipped down the lid on the toilet and sat,

even though the room really didn't have enough space for the two of them. But it did mean she didn't have a lot of room for escape.

"We did get a little carried away that night." Understatement of the century. It was the only time in his life, except for the first time with her all those years ago, when he hadn't given a thought to protection.

She tapped her hand on her opposite arm. "I have an implant. The never-fail birth control because you never fail to forget it."

It took him a minute to identify the sensation inside him, because it should have been relief and it wasn't.

She'd lowered her head again to rest on her knees and he started to touch her curls, but drew his fingers into a fist instead and pressed it to his thigh.

"That's good," he lied. "Would've had to marry you."

She didn't look at him, but her scoffing sound was more than clear. "You're not the marrying kind."

"Maybe not. There's only one girl who ever made me consider it."

She finally raised her head. Her face was still pale, but at least it wasn't ashen the way it had been earlier. Her lashes were lowered, keeping him from seeing her eyes. "What happened?"

He shrugged. "She threw her lot in with some-one else. You're sure you're not—"

"I'm *not*. Besides, just because a man is a hus-band, it doesn't necessarily follow that he's a good father. My own is proof of that."

"Montrose says you've thrown up more than once."

She finally gave him a look. "Montrose would never."

"The fact that he didn't confirm it was confir-mation enough."

She maneuvered herself around until she could push to her feet, but had to use his shoulder as le-verage in the confining space. "You shove your career in a cement mixer for a while and see if it doesn't cause you enough stress to throw up a few times." She opened the crackled-mirror cabinet above the sink and pulled out a bottle of mouth-wash. She swished some in her mouth, spat it out and returned the bottle to its spot. Then without looking at him, she sidled around his legs again and left.

He followed her back into the kitchen, where the dough was now resting inside an oval basket. Montrose was wiping up the flour covering the counter.

"I think I can take it from here," Nell was tell-ing him as she tugged the cloth from his resistant hand. "Thanks."

"Once it's doubled, you punch it down and let it rise again."

"I know. I remember." Archer felt as if he was hallucinating when she tucked her arm through the other man's and maneuvered him out of the kitchen. "I'll bring you pictures tomorrow to show you the results."

"Bring the *loaf*," Montrose ordered. "I've made fresh jam to go with it."

Then he heard the door shut and a moment later, Nell returned to the kitchen. She picked up the cloth and started scrubbing at the flour still stuck on the faded pink-and-gray countertop.

"He has fresh jam."

"And I hope it's something pedestrian like good old strawberry and not weird like caviar basil or God knows what." She gave a quick shake of her head.

"I wish you'd have told me about Martin," he said quietly.

She didn't pretend to misunderstand. "And let you know how blind I was?" She had one hand braced on the counter as she scrubbed with the other, her springy hair bouncing around her shoulders. It was longer than it had been a few weeks ago.

"Why did you wait so long to report it?"

Her shoulders sagged and she stopped scrubbing. She angled her chin and looked at him.

"Ros."

She moved to the sink, a set expression on her face. "You're not the only one who protects her." She flipped on the water and rinsed her cloth. "For all the good it'll do if he's actually censured, too."

"You don't know for sure that *you* will be."

"I should be." She threw the cloth down into the sink and it hit with a wet splat.

He settled his hand on her back, right between her too-sharp shoulder blades. He felt her flinch but she didn't move away. He spread his fingers upward to the base of her neck, where her muscles felt as tight as his, and he turned her toward him into his embrace.

He'd expected resistance. But instead, she actually leaned against him. Her arms slid around his shoulders and she pressed her forehead against his neck. He could feel the sigh she gave throughout her entire body.

He kissed the top of her head. But he didn't dare do anything more because he'd already proved that he had too little control where she was concerned. "It's going to be all right. We'll get through this. One step at a time."

She didn't say anything. But her arms tightened around him. "I can't believe you remembered I wanted a bookstore like my mother's," she mumbled against him.

He closed his eyes. "I remember everything."

Her head moved, but only, it seemed, to burrow deeper against him. "I asked Greer to feed your cat," she finally said.

He smiled faintly and brushed a kiss against her hair one more time.

Nell stared at the plastic stick in her hand.

Two lines for positive.

One line for negative.

And there were absolutely two fat, pink lines.

The test she'd done the day before had given the same results.

And the one before that, also the same.

She lifted her arm to glare at the spot where she knew the tiny implant was located. "So much for you."

She dropped her arm and tossed the pregnancy test stick into the trash along with its two twins and eyed her reflection in the crackled mirror over her sink.

Did she look different?

Her face didn't. As long as nobody paid any attention to her breasts that seemed to have outgrown their usual cup size overnight, her body didn't look any different, either.

She pressed her hand to her stomach. "Not yet, anyway."

Her eyes suddenly stung.

It was an annoyance that had been happening with increasing frequency the last few weeks.

She'd gotten teary over the library site being finalized. Over her fifth failed attempt to bake a decent loaf of bread despite Montrose's tutelage. She'd even cried over the unexpected phone call she'd received from Gardner, who'd called to ask Nell for advice about the best way to protect her boys should something ever happen to her.

Her knees felt as watery as her eyes and she sank down on the closed toilet lid.

How was she going to tell Archer when not even two weeks ago she'd sat in this very bathroom insisting there was no possible way for her to be pregnant?

That's good. Would've had to marry you.

His words echoed inside her head.

As soon as he'd said them—before she'd even given any thought to the possibility that her implant might have become too old to be effective— she'd realized that the only proposal she would ever want from him was one *not* prompted by a baby in her belly.

She was in love with Archer Templeton.

And she feared she had been for a very, very long time.

Nausea clawed at her and she leaned over the sink, running cold water over the insides of her wrists until it began to subside.

They were supposed to be giving their workshop at the wellness expo that afternoon. He was picking her up because he was coming all the way from Cheyenne anyway after he'd spent the last few days in meetings at the state capitol building.

Considering the frequency of her bouts of nausea, she didn't know how she was going to make it through the drive to Braden, much less the afternoon-long workshop they'd be conducting, without him noticing.

That's good. Would've had to marry you.

She made an impatient sound and turned off the water. She mopped the mascara smudges from around her eyes, pulled on the soft pink biker-style jacket that Delia had talked her into buying at Classic Charms a few days earlier to go with her black jeans and left the bathroom just in time to hear a truck engine out front.

Her stomach lurched, but this time it wasn't because of nausea. It was simply pure nervousness.

She opened the front door to wave at Archer, then ducked back inside. She went into the second bedroom, where she'd set up a small table and enough shelves to house her collection of books, and picked up the stack of stapled packets she'd been preparing in her spare time for the workshop.

Archer had told her that his office in Denver could have taken care of it, but if she'd agreed, she wouldn't have felt like she was contributing anything to what was supposed to be their combined effort.

It was hard enough being ineffectual while waiting for the bar's decision regarding her future as a lawyer. She didn't need to feel useless where everything else was concerned, too.

She shouldered her briefcase strap and with her arms full of the packets, went back out to the living room. As usual, bells jangled inside her at the sight of him, tall and gold and crazily handsome, as he walked through her front door and set a stack of mail on the little table she'd placed there so she'd have a spot to dump her keys when she came in every day.

Like her, he was wearing black jeans. His white shirt was rolled up at the elbows and open at the neck. His jaw was clean-shaven and his hair was slicked back and if she hadn't vowed not to repeat the mistake that had gotten her into her latest predicament, she'd have been busily wondering if she possessed what it would take to seduce him.

But she *had* vowed, and she was not in the market to do anything such thing.

So she summarily dumped the packets into his hands. "I just have another box of handouts to grab." She frowned when he set the packets on the small table, as well.

There wasn't a single trace of amusement in

his deep green gaze. Not a hint of a dimple in his lean cheeks.

"What's wrong?"

He pulled a thin envelope from his back pocket.

There was no postage stamp on the corner and she recognized the seal on the front of it and felt her nerves pinch. "Have you become an official deliveryman now for the bar association?"

"They knew I was seeing you. Instead of making you wait for it to come by mail…" He held it out but when she went to reach for it, he tipped it out of her grasp. "I know you don't want to wait to see what it says, but there's something I need to—" He broke off and cleared his throat. "Just… just wait a minute before you decide to open it up."

She frowned even harder and her alarm grew. It was rare to see him looking so… She didn't even have a word for it. *Uncomfortable* wasn't quite right. Neither was *uncertain*.

"Why?"

"Because I…well, hell." He turned to the stuff on the table and sent the stack of packets careening onto the floor. He muttered an oath and if she weren't mistaken, a dusky tide of color was rising up his throat as he tried and failed to catch them.

She had to bite the inside of her cheek to keep from smiling, because as alarmed as she was feeling inside, it was seriously, *seriously* gratifying to see him have to fumble. Just once. Just a little.

She set down her briefcase and crouched next to him, gathering up the thick packets. Some had even landed outside the open door. She leaned on her hand and reached past him to get them, then sat back on her heels and dropped them onto the untidy pile he'd managed to gather. "Want to tell me what's going on here or should I start making guesses?"

"You wouldn't guess this." He dumped the packets back onto the table, then straightened and took her hands and pulled her to her feet. "Maybe you should sit."

Her mouth went dry. "Is Vivian all right?" His grandmother had returned from Philadelphia the week before without offering any explanations for her abrupt trip. Nell could only assume she'd been seeing doctors despite Delia's claim otherwise.

His brows jerked together. "Yeah. Yeah. She's fine."

Nell sank down on the edge of the couch. She'd bought it from Classic Charms. It was second-hand, but it was a pretty shade of blue and comfortable to boot. "Then *what*?"

"Martin's facing federal charges on bribery and extortion," he said abruptly. Bluntly. "He was arrested early this morning."

Her jaw dropped.

Archer crouched in front of her, his hands

clasping hers. "He might not pay the price for anything else, but he's going to pay the price for this."

"But how…what?" She could hardly comprehend it. "Does Ros know? Have you talked to Meredith?"

"Yes. And yes. I saw Ros for a few minutes before I started heading up here. Needless to say, the law firm's going to be picked apart before long. Investigations like that tend to spawn more. She's pretty shaken up."

Nell's eyes dampened. "I can imagine. I hope Jonathan is with her."

He made a face. "I think they already split up a while ago. Meredith and my dad are on their way to Cheyenne. I don't know if Ros will be all that ready to see them, but they're going to try."

Her eyes flooded with more tears. "I can't believe it." She swiped her cheek. "Where's the letter you brought for me?"

He took it back out of his pocket and set it beside her on the couch. "There's more."

"I'm not sure my nerves can handle more." She picked up the envelope and slid her finger beneath the sealed flap.

"What about your heart?"

She stared. "What?"

His throat had that dusky color again. "This is one of those when-it-rains-it-pours times." He got up again and went back to the table by the door, fumbling through the mess until he pulled out another envelope.

This one was thicker. Larger. And when he handed it to her, she could immediately feel that it contained a book.

"I should have given it to you a long time ago." He rubbed his fingers through his hair, looking oddly embarrassed. "I planned to. But things didn't turn out the way I thought they would, and—"

"Archer, what on earth are you talking about?"

"Just open it."

Her heart was suddenly chugging inside her chest, pushing up into her throat. She pulled open the flap and tipped the book out onto her lap.

The dust jacket was glossy. In perfect condition except for the small tear in one corner.

She traced a shaking finger over the fat little penguin on the cover. *"Monty Meets Mary,"* she whispered. Her mother's tenth book. The only one she had never been able to find.

A tear splashed on the cover and she slowly wiped it away.

"It was in a used-book store in Montana. Total coincidence that I found it." He shrugged, still looking uncomfortable. Uncertain. "I'd gotten in the habit of always looking for one of her books whenever I saw a used-book store. I was going to give it to you when you passed the bar. When I—"

"That long?" She swiped her cheeks. "You've had it that long? Why didn't you—" She broke off, because it didn't matter how long he'd had it. "It doesn't matter." She pressed the book to her heart. "Thank you."

"You didn't let me finish." He crouched in front of her again and took her hand and her heart lurched all over again at the realization that *his* hand wasn't entirely steady. "What I was saying was that I was going to give it to you when I asked you to marry me."

She went still. Her eyes felt trapped in his gaze.

He slowly reached out to draw a curl away from her face. "I didn't want you just to be my partner back then, Cornelia. You were the girl I wanted. The girl I wanted to be my wife. I still—"

"You were seeing someone else. One of the professors. Ros told me."

He looked pained. "You think she wanted to share her best friend with the stepbrother she couldn't stand?"

"I never told her about us!"

"I did."

"What?"

He scrubbed his hand down his face. When his gaze met hers again, his eyes were steady. "I know there's no point trying to whitewash my own behavior. I knew you wanted to join Martin's firm more than anything. Ros knew it, too, and she liked tossing that fact at me just because she knew how much it stung. So I told her about us just so she'd shut up."

"She never said anything to me."

"She wouldn't, would she?"

"So she lied to me about the professor?"

"It wasn't a lie. It was just information that was a couple years too old. And don't be mad at her for being foolish. We were all foolish then."

She was trembling. "You had an affair with one of the professors while *you* were still in school."

"Does it matter now? It was a long time ago. Before I fell in love with you."

She pressed the book harder against her breast, feeling his words quaking inside her. "I fell in love with you, too," she whispered.

"And now? Because you didn't let me finish again. I still want you to be my wife, Nell." He flicked his finger against the envelope lying on the couch beside her. "Regardless of what that says. I'm sick of pretending. Sick of waiting." He pressed his lips for a moment to the back of her hand that he still held. "Everything that's happened since you danced on that bar in Cheyenne and landed in my arms has made me face that fact. I want you as my partner. As my lover. And maybe—" His jaw canted for a moment.

When he spoke again, his voice was husky.

"And maybe one day you *will* be pregnant. Because you want to have my child as much I do."

There was a river of tears running down her face and she couldn't do a thing to stop it. She decided that was just what had to happen when a heart was too full.

She stood, still clasping *Monty Meets Mary* with one hand and Archer with her other. "Come." She pulled him into her spare bedroom and carefully slid the book into place on the shelf next to number nine. "This is number eleven." She pulled it out and placed it in his hands. *"Monty Marries Mary."* She kissed him slowly. "Yes. I want you to be my husband."

He started to reach for her but she shook her head. "Wait." She pulled out the last of her mother's books. "This is number twelve," she said huskily. "The final story." She slowly placed it in his hands, feeling herself sinking into his green gaze. *"Monty and Mary Have a Baby."*

His pupils dilated a little. "You want to have a baby?" He sounded disbelieving. "With me?"

She leaned into him and brushed her lips against his. "What I'm trying to tell you is that I am *having* your baby. With you."

His head jerked up.

His eyes searched hers. A sparkle suddenly glinted somewhere deep inside. "Really?"

She threaded her fingers through his and pressed them against her abdomen. "Really."

He dropped right then and there onto his knees and pressed his mouth against their joined hands. "I wish I had a diamond ring," he said fervently. No hint of disbelief anymore? "It would feel more official with a ring."

She suddenly felt like laughing. Because that's something a person also did when their heart was so full.

She threaded her fingers through his hair and kissed his forehead. His cheeks. His mouth. She had a vague thought about the workshop that they were still going to need to give. About the contents of the letter from the bar association. About Ros and how they were going to have to find some way to be there for her, too, because she was going to need them.

But for now, for at least these few minutes, and for the rest of their lives, they had *this*.

"You brought me *Monty Meets Mary*," she whispered. "And that, my impossible, beautiful Archer, is dearer to me than any diamond in the entire world."

* * * * *

If you loved
Nell and Archer,
don't miss the next
Return to the Double-C story,

Something about the Season

by New York Times
bestselling author
Allison Leigh

Coming November 2020
Exclusively from
Harlequin Special Edition.

**WE HOPE YOU ENJOYED
THIS BOOK FROM**

HARLEQUIN
SPECIAL
EDITION

Believe in love. Overcome obstacles. Find happiness.

Relate to finding comfort and strength in the
support of loved ones and enjoy the journey
no matter what life throws your way.

6 NEW BOOKS AVAILABLE EVERY MONTH!

COMING NEXT MONTH FROM

H HARLEQUIN

SPECIAL EDITION

Available August 18, 2020

#2785 THE MAVERICK'S BABY ARRANGEMENT
Montana Mavericks: What Happened to Beatrix?
by Kathy Douglass
In order to retain custody of his eight-month-old niece, Daniel Dubois convinces event planner and confirmed businesswoman Brittany Brandt to marry him. It's only supposed to be a mutually beneficial business agreement...*if* they can both keep their hearts out of the equation.

#2786 THE LAST MAN SHE EXPECTED
Welcome to Starlight • by Michelle Major
When Mara Reed agrees to partner with her sworn enemy, Parker Johnson, to help a close friend, she doesn't expect the feelings of love and tenderness that complicate every interaction with the handsome attorney. Will Mara and Parker risk everything for love?

#2787 CHANGING HIS PLANS
Gallant Lake Stories • by Jo McNally
Real estate developer Brittany Doyle is eager to bring the mountain town of Gallant Lake into the twenty-first century...by changing everything. Hardware store owner Nate Thomas hates change. These opposites refuse to compromise, except when it comes to falling in love.

#2788 A WINNING SEASON
Wickham Falls Weddings • by Rochelle Alers
When Sutton Reed returns to Wickham Falls after finishing a successful baseball career, he assumes he'll just join the family business and live an uneventful life. Until his neighbor's younger brother tries to steal his car, that is. Now he's finding himself mentoring the boy—and being drawn to Zoey Allen like no one else.

#2789 IN SERVICE OF LOVE
Sutter Creek, Montana • by Laurel Greer
Commitmentphobic veterinarian Maggie is focused on training a Great Dane as a service dog and expanding the family dog-training business. Can widowed single dad Asher's belief in love after loss inspire Maggie to risk her heart and find forever with the irresistible librarian?

#2790 THE SLOW BURN
Masterson, Texas • by Caro Carson
When firefighter Caden Sterling unexpectedly delivers Tana McKenna's baby by the side of the road, the unlikely threesome forms a special bond. Their flirty friendship slowly becomes more, until Tana's ex and the truth about her baby catches up with her. Can she win back the only man who can make this family complete?

YOU CAN FIND MORE INFORMATION ON UPCOMING HARLEQUIN TITLES, FREE EXCERPTS AND MORE AT HARLEQUIN.COM.

HSECNM0820

*Real estate developer Brittany Doyle is eager to
bring the mountain town of Gallant Lake into the
twenty-first century...by changing everything.
Hardware store owner Nate Thomas hates change.
These opposites refuse to compromise, except when it
comes to falling in love.*

Read on for a sneak peek at
Changing His Plans,
*the next book in the Gallant Lake Stories
miniseries by Jo McNally.*

He stuck his head around the corner of the fasteners
aisle just in time to see a tall brunette stagger into the
revolving seed display. Some of the packets went flying,
but she managed to steady the display before the whole
thing toppled. He took in what probably had been a very
nice silk blouse and tailored trouser suit before she was
drenched in the storm raging outside. The heel on one of
the ridiculously high heels she was wearing had snapped
off, explaining why she was stumbling around.

"Having a bad morning?"

The woman looked up in annoyance, strands of dark,
wet hair falling across her face.

"You could say that. I don't suppose you have a shoe
repair place in this town?" She looked at the bright red
heel in her hand.

HSEEXP0820

Nate shook his head as he approached her. "Nope. But hand it over. I'll see what I can do."

A perfectly shaped brow arched high. "Why? Are you going to cobble them back together with—" she gestured around widely "—maybe some staples or screws?"

"Technically, what you just described is the definition of cobbling, so yeah. I've got some glue that'll do the trick." He met her gaze calmly. "It'd be a lot easier to do if you'd take the shoe off. Unless you also think I'm a blacksmith?"

He was teasing her. Something about this soaking-wet woman still having so much…regal bearing…amused Nate. He wasn't usually a fan of the pearl-clutching country club set who strutted through Gallant Lake on the weekends and referred to his family's hardware store as "adorable." But he couldn't help admiring this woman's ability to hold on to her superiority while looking like she accidentally went to a water park instead of the business meeting she was dressed for. To be honest, he also admired the figure that expensive red suit was clinging to as it dripped water on his floor.

He held out his hand. "I'm Nate Thomas. This is my store."

She let out an irritated sigh. "Brittany Doyle." She slid her long, slender hand into his and gripped with surprising strength. He held it for just a half second longer than necessary before shaking off the odd current of interest she invoked in him.

Don't miss
Changing His Plans *by Jo McNally,*
available September 2020 wherever
Harlequin Special Edition books and ebooks are sold.

Harlequin.com